FAKING THE
HARMONY

Maddie Evans

Print ISBN: 978-1-942133-41-4
Library of Congress Control Number: 2020948509

Cover art by Crowe Covers
Editing by Michelle Arnold

DEDICATION

Some random stranger was chatting with my mother and said, "I know there are a lot of great violinists in the world, but the greatest violinist who ever lived was Angelo Consoli. I'm sure you never heard of him."
My mother exclaimed, "Are you kidding? He was my uncle!"

Uncle Angelo, I am honored to have had a few violin lessons in the kitchen of the greatest violinist who ever lived. I was just a kid and had no idea what I was doing. As opposed to now as an adult, when I still have no idea what I'm doing.

CHAPTER ONE

Rose pounded out the final notes of "Daybreak Nightfall," closing chords that served as the payoff of all the themes buried in the opening. The four members of Clear Enigma had hammered on this finale for the past hour and they were so close to nailing it. So close—

The drummer gave an audible cue, and they all crescendoed to a stop.

"Whoa!" Bass guitarist Corwin pumped his fist in the air. "Great job, everyone!" He pointed at Rose. "Brilliant! You are brilliant, and you have brilliant ideas."

Sean, their vocalist and lead guitarist, raked a hand through his hair. "I still don't like that Raf has to disrupt the rhythm to give the closing cue."

"It happens so close to the end that it becomes part of the finale." Corwin looked to their drummer. "Maybe the cue could feel more like a part of the crescendo, but I thought that was stellar." Back to Rose. "Now—about the keyboard."

Rose arched her eyebrows. "This isn't just your band."

Sean snorted. "It is totally his band."

Raf stretched. "I don't care whose band it is. I'm calling it a night." He stepped away from the drums, and with that, practice was over.

They cleaned up the practice room in the basement of the Castleton School of Music, center of musical life in northern Maine. Or, in the case of Corwin Castleton, the center of his life. He was the youngest son of the music school's owners.

Sean looked at her while he set his guitar back in its case. "I didn't mean to be critical, Rose. That was a good idea to have Raf signal us to close by changing the rhythm."

Rose finished jotting notes on her sheet music. "I get it. The signal does disrupt the flow, but if we're jamming at the end and we all want to end at the same time—"

She stopped herself. Rehashing the argument for the ninetieth time wouldn't help even if they switched sides, her apologizing for her good idea and Sean apologizing for his reasonable objection.

Life had taught Rose that sometimes you just had to give up what you wanted and let the performance go on—a lesson driven home by the envelope in today's mail.

Corwin grabbed his bass guitar. "You all ready?" he said, as though he couldn't see they were. Everything went into the storage closet, and because he'd pretty much grown up in the music school, of course he had keys to lock up behind them.

It would be nice to lock a lot of things away, wouldn't it? Like, for example, that stupid envelope.

Corwin shut off the lights. "So—who else got an invite to Travis and Mia's wedding?"

Right on cue, the envelope.

Raf huffed. "Boycott that noise. Travis is a jerk, and Mia's no better."

Sean said, "I think I have to go. I've known Travis for

twenty years."

Corwin snickered. "You were in preschool together?"

Sean laughed. "Yeah, he was always my partner for building with blocks."

Rose sighed. "Guys, you don't have to skip out on a party because of me."

Corwin snorted. "Travis was a toad for the way he dumped you, and we all know Mia was on a campaign to steal him."

Rose said, "All of which happened eighteen months ago. I'm over him, and if Mia won the grand prize in the 'Toad Catching Contest,' more power to her."

That sounded awesome, didn't it? It wasn't totally a lie, either.

They reached the main floor, and Corwin dropped onto one of the lobby chairs. "Not the point. You're over him because you're a stand-up kind of person, but your awesomeness only makes his double-dealing worse because you didn't deserve it."

Raf leaned against the wall. "Not to mention, he tried to bust up the band."

With his hands in his pockets, Sean shrugged. "But that's why I'm even in the group. You wouldn't have replaced Travis with me if Travis hadn't left, so I can't find it in me to get too worked up."

Corwin shook his head. "Solidarity. It's a thing."

"It doesn't have to be a thing." Rose ran a hand through her hair. "There's no reason for you to sit it out. I just won't go."

Corwin did a double-take, and then his eyes narrowed. "Wait, they invited you? Now you have to go just to get revenge on her."

Rose rolled her eyes. "Mia had to invite me. Same deal as Sean: she's been my friend for ages."

Raf stared at the ceiling as though searching for enlightenment. "You guys in Hartwell need a refresher course on what friendship means."

"Yes, yes, you do everything better in New York City. I've

got it." Corwin folded his arms and crossed his legs at the ankle. "It's much easier when there's ten million people and you don't have to see the same faces every single time you go out in public. Hartwell is a petri dish, and the 'friend' options are much more limited."

Raf said, "In which case, wouldn't it behoove you Mainers not to abuse your so-called friends by stealing their boyfriends and breaking up their bands?"

Rose said, "That's a New York thing, right? Using *behoove* in a sentence?" and Raf gave her a big grin.

Corwin huffed. "If you recall, that's why we now have the no-dating-within-the-band rule."

"Which is unnecessary because as far as I know, none of us is interested in any of the other of us." Rose raised her hands. "I don't care if you go or do not go. *I* will not go."

Corwin said, "You're letting her win."

Rose said, "Let her win. First prize in the toad contest is still a toad."

From upstairs came footsteps, and Raf called, "Hey, Declan!"

Ah, Declan Hatcher. Tall, blue-eyed, and yet another person who'd rejected Rose. The stars must have lined up for a bad history parade.

Declan gave a wave to all four. "Clear Enigma, my favorite band!"

Corwin said, "Declan, my favorite liar!" and Declan laughed. Corwin added, "Let me know when you're ready to play interesting music."

"Will do. Let me know when you're ready to make money." Declan played jazz piano and had a Thursday night gig at a local bistro, as well as regular performances at dinner parties and weddings—all of which showed a strange reluctance to hire an alternative rock band. "Don't let me interrupt your argument."

Sean said, "Did you get invited to Travis Young's wedding? Everyone here got our invitations today."

Hartwell wasn't tiny like some of the towns around here, but it still felt like they were all up in one another's business all the time. One wedding, and everyone in their circle would have to attend so Mia could have hundreds of guests. She'd always been a "go big or go home" kind of girl, and now she'd become that kind of woman.

Mia had to have invited Declan. For a couple of years in high school, Mia had a massive crush on Declan, so surely she'd grab the opportunity to show off to him now.

Corwin added, "We're boycotting."

Rose sighed. "We're not boycotting because Sean's going, and I said I don't care."

Declan hesitated. "Oh, that's right, you used to date Travis."

Used to date Travis sounded so sterile. For two years, Rose had wrapped her world around Travis, daydreamed about Travis, spent every waking moment with Travis, and longed for a lifetime with Travis. A lifetime Travis said he wanted to spend with her, too—at least until he'd pulled away from her and started criticizing, started ignoring... started cheating.

And for what? For Mia? Except Travis and Mia were getting married, so it must have been good for him.

Rose only wished he'd broken up with her cleanly. Or that Travis would admit he'd cheated at all. (Everyone knew they'd cheated. Mia was gushing about her new boyfriend two days after the breakup, although Travis wouldn't admit to it until three months had passed. Three months of him appearing all over Hartwell with Mia, but don't bother him with facts.)

Corwin said, "Travis cheated on her, then tried to work his side dish into the band as a backup singer, which would be great except for her lack of talent. He made that his hill to die on, hence Travis is out, and Sean is in."

Sean raised his hands. "Living well is the best revenge. Go to the wedding and show them up. Head high."

Rose reached into her backpack for the invitation. "They don't want me there." She opened the inner envelope where it said, "Rosalind Ward and Guest," and underneath was a hand-written sticky note. *"I know you don't have anyone special, but maybe you can bring a second cousin or something?"*

Corwin's eyes flared. "Talk about petty! I need to up my game."

Raf snorted. "Rude. None of us even got plus ones, so she went out of her way to add that."

Sean said, "We could go as a group."

Rose shrugged. "She'll take it as the final victory if I show up single, and while I don't have a problem with being single, I hate having her lord it over me."

Declan said, "There's your answer. Which of you is dating Rose?"

Rose laughed out loud.

Declan swept a hand around the room. "You've got three guys in your band. Work with me. Pick one, and for a few hours at the reception, you two are fabulously in love."

"Sure, because Travis is totally stupid and doesn't remember how Corwin carved that 'No intra-band dating' rule in stone because of him." Rose shook her head. "You're trying to solve a problem that doesn't exist. Let her relish her magnificent victory. She wins a life with a cheater, and I win a life of being comfortable with my behavior."

Raf said, "You know that old adage? 'When a man marries his mistress, he creates a job opening,'" and Declan laughed hard.

"Next song I write, I'm calling it 'Second Cousin or Something.'" Corwin turned to Declan. "Declan, my dude, congratulations." In response to Declan's confusion, Corwin added, "Many happy returns on your blissful relationship with Rose."

"No, no, no!" Rose gave Declan the side-eye. "I am *most emphatically not his type.*"

Taking a step backward, Declan gave a nervous laugh.

Raf chucked him on the shoulder. "My dude. You just got roasted."

Sean rubbed his chin. "Now that sounds like you two have a history."

Even unnerved, Declan was just as cute now as he was back in high school when he'd burned Rose with those words. Rose flashed him her best performance smile. "No history, and there's no need for Declan to pretend he likes me. Living well is the best revenge. Mia had a petty laugh at my expense, but I don't care what Mia thinks."

Declan started. "Wait—Mia? Mia Pratt?" When Rose nodded, he folded his arms. "Deal me in. If escorting you to Mia's wedding will make her eat her heart out, I'm game."

Corwin brightened. "It's settled! Tell Mia you're bringing your wise second cousin Festus, and then on the day of, show up dressed to the nines on the arm of an adoring Declan."

"Guys, enough. She's a jerk, but I'd rather the marriage itself leads to slow misery rather than us ruining her wedding." Rose forced a smile. "The nastiest thing I ever did to her was to let her have Travis."

Declan's eyes narrowed. "She made my sister's life a living nightmare, and if I can return even part of the favor, I'm all for it."

Corwin urged, "Say yes, Rose. You'll be helping a man live his revenge fantasy."

"I appreciate it, but I don't need revenge." She picked up her backpack. "Declan, thanks anyway. It's awesome of you to offer to help."

Declan smiled, and it was a hint of a tease. "Any time— even though you're *quintessentially* not my type."

Chapter Two

Declan tightened his hands on the wheel. "You can stop laughing anytime now."

"You actually said that? She's *quintessentially not your type?*" Sean seemed disinclined to stop laughing. "And she didn't cut your head clean off at the shoulders?"

"My head's still attached because we weren't in the same place when I said it. You know how things happen in high school. She sent one of her friends to ask one of my friends whether I liked her, or maybe it was even more convoluted. That was my response, and somehow it either got back to her verbatim or it got back to her in the form she quoted it tonight." Declan snickered. "I'm surprised she even remembered."

"I'd be more surprised if she ever forgot. Maybe Corwin's second-to-next song should use that as the title." Sean hesitated. "What is your type, since she's quintessentially not it?"

Declan flinched. Yeah, about that. Rose was a little shorter than he preferred, considering he was six feet three, but as for the rest? Her short auburn hair bounced when she moved, and it looked inviting to his fingers. She had a soft palate voice that sounded awesome when she sang and would sound even better whispering in his ear. Even though she played a different style of music than he did, he admired her skill with a keyboard. Rose had a wicked sense of humor, and she picked up on subtle notes in conversations.

Declan wasn't sure he had a "type," but if he did, Rose would fit it.

Sean, however, wanted an answer. "I was sixteen. I'm not sure I knew what my type even was. She moved on. I never thought about it again."

Kind of. He'd kind of never thought about it again.

It wasn't as if he'd laid awake in the small dark hours, tormented by how he'd shut her down. He'd said those words precisely because he'd wanted to shut her down. That roundabout exchange had comprised almost the entire interaction between them: lots of semi-flirting during Castleton Music School events, her friends sussing out information from his friends, his friends teasing him about her...and finally the thirdhand overture and the rejection. For a couple of weeks, it had been awkward, until it hadn't anymore. Eventually their lives diverged. This year, Declan and Sean were sharing an apartment, meaning every so often Declan ran into her because of Clear Enigma.

And each time, Declan encountered once again the way in which Rose really wasn't his type: Rose thought she was better than him.

She'd been in full force this evening, with all three guys in her band defending her, and her refusing to acknowledge it. She didn't need them, didn't want their help, wouldn't consider anything.

She'd topped that off with her refusal of *Declan's* help, as though Declan were so beneath her that she couldn't stand the thought of his assistance. Not even to let him get even with the same person she wanted to show up.

They would have made a natural duet, her showing up her ex-boyfriend's affair partner and him striking back at the monster who'd savaged his sister's high school years. Instead, from the minute Rose had moved to Hartwell as a high school sophomore, she'd set herself on a pedestal, and all these years later she still hadn't stepped down.

Sean said, "Did high school stink for you as much as it did for me?"

Declan shook his head. "The biggest issues we had at Regional were people poking each other with soldering wires. Nothing near the drama I heard about in the Hartwell schools."

Sean sighed. "Small town, big drama."

The vo-tech high school's HVAC certification program had been fun, plus it led to year-round employment with benefits. A tech who worked his cards right could manage weekends and evenings free to play professional piano. There was nice money in heating and air conditioning, and there was nice work but little money in jazz piano. Between the two of them, Declan was set for life. Corwin had a similar setup, working as a welder to make money and as a musician to make life worthwhile.

At home, Sean cobbled something together for dinner while Declan went to his room and texted his sister. "Today I very nearly got vengeance on your behalf."

Kimi texted back, "Do tell! I love a good revenge tragedy."

"The tragedy is that I won't be able to do it."

Kimi sent him a sad-faced emoji. "Exactly what revenge are we talking about?"

"Mia the Monster cheated with Travis Young, and now they're getting married. Cor Castleton says Mia will get jealous if I escort Travis's ex to the wedding, but she refused."

Kimi sent back, "Good for her. It sounds like a mess."

Declan added, "Mia wrote a rude note on her invitation."

Kimi texted, "Some people never change."

Declan replied, "If she'd said yes, I could have avenged you too."

Kimi sent a smiling emoji. "Stay out of this. My revenge is how Mia will live the rest of her life being exactly who she is."

"Fitting punishment," Declan replied.

For that matter, Rose would also live the rest of her life being who she was: queen of the mountain, and too proud ever to descend.

CHAPTER THREE

One of the waitresses sidled over to Rose with, "They're back."

Rose groaned, not even needing to ask who *they* were in this context. It would have to be Mia and her younger sister Allison, both of whom dropped by the Hartwell Diner on a regular basis. They were the only people in town who got waited on by a manager because none of the waitstaff were allowed to deal with them any longer—which was exactly what Mia and Mia-junior wanted. They certainly weren't coming for the three-egg special.

Muttering, "What I wouldn't do to work for someone with a backbone," Rose went to take their order.

Mia had caught Rose's approach in her peripheral vision because she started showing off her diamond engagement ring to her sister. "I'm so *blessed* and *lucky* to have a guy who loves me this much!"

That note about the "second cousin" burned in Rose's

brain as she set their menus on the table. The diner hadn't bothered updating its menu since the Carter presidency, but Mia demanded a menu every time. A roaring 20's theme dominated the walls, so the meals had names like "flapper jacks" because that was kitschy enough to keep the summertime tourists smiling. "Coffee for both of you?"

"Is it fresh? I don't want it if it's not fresh." Mia-junior's nose wrinkled. "Can you wait until you brew a fresh pot and pour it right out?"

"Actually, pull the pot before the whole thing brews so it's stronger." Mia smiled. "Otherwise it's too weak."

They sell coffee up the street, you know. If Rose ever said that, she'd lose her job. "Of course. Do you know what you want this morning?"

Rose had made the mistake of a passive-aggressive remark two months ago, but as the queen of passive-aggressive, Mia had seized on it with the thrill of victory. She'd wept to Larry, the diner's owner, about Rose appointing herself the food police. Rose had endured five excruciating minutes considering how everyone would laugh about her getting fired from a job as uninspiring as managing a diner...and then somehow she'd escaped with her job. On the way back from Mia's table, though, Larry had murmured, "Don't comment again on their orders."

Nor could she comment on their snippy pot-shots about how Mia was able to lock down the man Rose hadn't.

Rose dumped extra grounds into a filter. Mia made the same request every time: she wanted the fresh coffee as it poured through the fresh grounds because those drips were the strongest. Neither she nor Larry listened to Rose's objection that doing this left the rest of the pot weaker for everyone else. Nor did Mia want espresso. Mister Spineless Larry just muttered, "Go on and do it," but how many customers wouldn't complain and also wouldn't return? You couldn't win back someone's good opinion once you'd ruined it. Not in real life, but especially not in the restaurant business.

Therefore Rose worked around the constraints of both her spineless boss and her selfish ex-friend: she added too much coffee at the beginning, hijacked the first two cups right out of the stream, and ensured the rest would be nearly right. It took five minutes, but then she was out with two extra-strong and perfectly-fresh coffees.

"It always takes so long," Mia murmured, ignoring that it was her own fault. "I suppose you're doing your best."

You have no idea. "They'll have your omelets out in a few minutes."

Mia's whole setup—the fresh coffee, a private server—was her reward for bad behavior. She'd complained about the morning servers one after the next until Larry decreed only Rose could wait Mia's table. Mia abused Rose until Larry capitulated just to get her to shut up. Oh, and Mia was marrying Travis, the ultimate reward for bad behavior.

Mia hadn't brought up the wedding invitation, giving Rose a chance to be preemptively mean so Mia could complain. Again. It wasn't enough to take Rose's man. She also wanted to take Rose's job.

Mia wouldn't want Rose's job anyhow. Mia worked reception in a salon, which gave her free mornings, access to high-quality products, plus long stretches between phone calls to page through bridal magazines.

In the kitchen, Rose did paperwork until Mia and her sister finished up. The only good thing Rose would say about them was they tipped well, although Mia wrote condescending notes on her receipt. "Have you ever thought of mascara? We have some on sale this week."

You won, Rose thought as she tallied inventory in the walk-in. *Take your victory and leave.*

Finally, Rose presented the check. (Mia had complained about the other waitstaff "dropping" the check, so Rose always made sure to "present" it.) A few minutes more and they'd be out of her diner. The two waitresses could share a collective (and secretive) eye-roll in the kitchen, and they'd go back to serving good coffee to their good customers.

Mia raised her eyebrows. "Did you get my invitation? A dozen people said their invitations arrived yesterday, and they're all telling me how pretty they are! I had to work for hours with the printer to make sure the embossing was right, and it took three attempts to get a shade of coral that matched my bridesmaids' dresses."

What good is a sticky-note insult if you aren't there to gloat over it hitting home? *A second cousin or something.* It would serve Mia right if Rose picked up a hitchhiker as her plus-one. "No, sir, please don't bother to bathe. It's fine if your jeans are caked in mud. In fact, I'd prefer you come just as you are."

Rose couldn't do something like that. Who would they blame? The bride, who'd extended an olive branch to her new husband's ex-girlfriend? Or would they blame the vindictive ex for ruining the bride's special day?

Instead Rose made a show of brightening up. "Are you inviting me? Isn't that sweet of you! Who's doing the music?"

Mia-junior smirked, but not at Rose. Nice to know Mia was surrounded by people as shallow as she was.

Even with her low blow thwarted, Mia kept her composure. "Well, our band is just so thrilled about the wedding that our second vocalist is donating his services as a soloist during the wedding ceremony."

"How wonderful," said Rose, rather than, "How exploitative!"

Mia said, "As for the reception, we've hired a live band," which turned out to be one of the local bands Rose knew from the Castleton Music School.

Please, let these two leave. Please. "That sounds amazing. I'm so glad it's all coming together for you."

Mia-junior prompted, "But not for you, right? You haven't dated anyone since Travis dumped you."

For the past two years, Rose had tried flirting with a couple of guys, but they'd ghosted her. She'd dated one man for a few months, but he wasn't a musician. Although he liked dating "a rock star," he didn't like music, so without any connection, the early glow had guttered out.

Rose forced a smile. "Everything came together fine for me, but thanks."

Mia said, "You're still working the same job, though, and you're with the same band. I feel so badly that you haven't moved on."

Rose enjoyed her job, and Clear Enigma would have been good enough for Mia to join it. Mia was so good at reversing the victim and the offender, so good at pointing to green and calling it red. Mia had worked at four salons in two years. Was that supposed to be a positive?

Rose shrugged. "Why would I move on from things I like doing?"

Mia leaned in. "But you're still alone, right? At the end of the day, you go home, and there's nobody. I used to be the same and thought it was fine, but now that I've found real love, I see how empty it all was. I was jealous because I thought you had the perfect life. I wanted nothing more than the chance to create music and a life with a wonderful man, and it looked like you had it all. But now that I have it, I see you didn't really have it at all. And I feel so bad for you."

Rose's grip tightened on the pen in her pocket. "Actually, I do have someone in my life, and there's no need to feel bad."

Mia-junior straightened. "Who?"

Rose forced the most insincere smile she'd done since the high school play where she'd had to kiss Freddie Johnson. "Declan Hatcher."

Mia laughed. "Well, he must be desperate. I thought you were 'most explicitly not his type.'"

"*Quintessentially*," Rose corrected. "We laugh about that now. But I'm so happy to hear that you keep thinking about me." She stepped back. "I'll take the check whenever you're ready," and she sauntered to the kitchen with a little swing in her hips.

As the door shut behind her, Rose pulled out her cell phone. Declan....Declan... Did she even have his number?

Yes, it was in a group chat. So help her, he and she had never even texted, but now they were going to be in love.

Second cousin, as if. Try having me sitting in front of you, kissing a guy you were massively crushing on in high school.

Rose texted, "Declan, I changed my mind. I'd like to take you up on that offer."

CHAPTER FOUR

Declan arrived to find Rose at her door, eyes averted. "Hey, thanks for coming over." Looking timid, she stepped back to let him cross the threshold.

"Nice place." Welcome to the world of Miss Neat-and-Color-Coordinated. Rose and her apartment-mate shared a townhome apartment in one of those complexes with names like Fuzzy Maples, whereas Declan and Sean lived in a house that had seen both world wars only to get carved into four units about thirty years ago. If you opened a bag of marbles in Declan's kitchen, they'd all roll into the bathroom. Most of Declan and Sean's furniture had spent at least one afternoon sitting curbside during a college town's move-out day. By contrast, either Rose or her apartment-mate had strung twinkle lights across the walls and installed tiny shelves arranged with knickknacks.

In the living room, he paused in front of a lever harp gilded with Celtic knots. "Yours?"

"Sierra's."

As far as Hartwell was concerned, there was only one Sierra: Corwin's sister. Declan resisted the temptation to pluck the strings. "I didn't realize you two roomed together."

"For about a year now. Do you want something to drink? Hot chocolate, maybe? Tea? Soda?"

Whoa, pulling out all the stops. "I'm good, thanks." Declan followed Rose through the cream-and-peach toned living room to a kitchen with white cabinets and an empty dish rack. He took a chair at the gleaming butcher-block table, and she sat opposite.

"Thanks for doing this," she added, as though she hadn't said that right from the start. She wouldn't meet his eyes, and Declan fought annoyance at the faux-humility of Princess Rose condescending to speak to her hired man. Declan was there to do a job. He didn't require fawning.

He leaned back in his chair. "What made you change your mind?"

"Mia." She looked up, fire in her eyes. Anger was a good look on her, much better than the polished jitters. "She sauntered into the diner and wanted nothing more than to have me freak out. I have zero interest in giving her the satisfaction. I pretended I hadn't gotten the invite, so she told me how much she pitied me for being alone in the world. I informed her I was together with you." Rose flinched. "And then I thought, maybe you ought to know...?"

Declan finally relaxed. Two scores settled for the price of one. First, they had Mia as their primary target, but second, he now had the personal satisfaction of Rose knowing he was her only way out of the jam she'd gotten herself into.

"I told you I was in if you wanted me, but that's why we need to work out the ground rules." Of course, as soon as he'd sent that response, Rose had jumped at the chance to make him come to her place. In her territory, she'd feel superior. She'd get the kitchen sparkling and offer him an herbal tea, and by doing so, she'd re-assert her dominance.

Rose folded her hands, disarmed and surprisingly cute. "I wasn't sure what you meant by that. All either one of us has to do is show up, sit together, maybe dance together."

Declan said, "Also drive there together."

Rose frowned. Annoyingly, that was cute too. He was going to have to be careful or he'd forget the enormous gap she'd put between them. She said, "Did you come over tonight so we could compare our vehicles for maximum impact? Or should we pool our funds and rent a limo?"

Declan laughed. This was a little dangerous now that she was putting some spark into the conversation. "You've seen what I drive."

"Jeep Grand Cherokee? That would pair awesome with my silver heels."

Declan nodded. "We could take it mudding before the ceremony to set the mood."

"You're such a romantic. The trouble is, you do have the better vehicle. I drive a pickup."

Declan's eyes widened.

Rose pointed at him. "No! I will not help you move."

Declan drummed his fingers on the table. "I hadn't even asked yet. These negotiations are the worst."

Rose arched her eyebrows, snickering. "Since my truck is now excluded from the negotiations, are you about to pick up your toys and leave?"

"It's not even worth it if I can't haul stuff. But if you insist, item one on the agreement is that your truck is off limits, and I'll drive us around in my Jeep. After we've gone mudding."

Rose offered, "I can pay for the car wash after."

"You will do no such thing. Item two on the agenda, we each pay our own way. I will put gas in the Jeep to get to and from the wedding."

She rested her chin on her folded hands and fluttered her eyes. "Aren't you just a chivalrous knight! Ponying up for a car wash *and* a full tank?"

His throat went unexpectedly warm. "Item three," he

said, struggling to come up with something before her smoky eyes distracted him, "we can go together on a gift for the happy couple, but we should discuss the budget ahead of time."

Rose pouted. "I was going to order ten thousand feeder crickets."

Declan shook his head. "While I appreciate the sentiment, I don't think Travis or Mia have a bearded dragon."

Rose had a perfect deadpan. "I know."

"The point is to kill them with kindness, not with a plague of locusts." Declan paused. "On the other hand, they'll be getting so many gifts delivered that an anonymous package might just get opened..."

"If someone does that, I'll be the first person they blame." Rose hesitated. "I'd better head off Corwin before he does something like that."

That drew Declan up short. "I hadn't considered Corwin. I know he disagrees, but living well really is the best revenge."

Rose didn't look inspired. Then, hesitant, she looked at her folded hands. "I hate to bring this up, but to make it convincing—"

Ah, that. "Item four addresses physical contact. What would you feel comfortable with?"

Rose glanced at him from under her thick hair. "Hand-holding? Arms around shoulders?"

That teasing look was a serve, and Declan gave a sly smile as his swing. "Should we print a diagram of the human body and start X-ing off parts?"

Rose lowered her eyes to look even more sultry. "If a bathing suit would cover it, don't touch it. I know the rules."

Suddenly it was hard not to think about the things Declan could do that wouldn't involve bathing suit territory. Hands up the back of her neck into that thick hair. His lips tucked into the hollow of her throat to nuzzle her soft skin. And her, with her eyes closed, her head tilted just a bit, her breathing punctuated.

He shifted in the seat. "Have you ever performed as the love interest in a play?"

Her nose wrinkled. "Yes, unfortunately. You?"

Declan said, "No, but since you've done it, you can stage a convincing performance. Like the way when you're playing with Clear Enigma, you look angry all the time."

Anger really was a good look for her. She rewarded him now with an irritated glance. "When you're performing, you look..."

When she cut herself off, Declan opened his hands. "You have to finish that sentence."

She shrank back. "You look like you're working hard. You're not really there."

Declan huffed. "I'm pretty sure I'm there."

"But your brain isn't there. It's off in the piano somewhere, monitoring every last vibration. If someone came up behind you with an axe and lopped off your head, you wouldn't notice until it occurred to you that you couldn't hear the notes any longer."

That was...well, very nearly accurate. Declan said, "Meaning?"

"Meaning, if you're working that hard to convince people we're together, they'll know you're working hard to do it."

"Then we need to practice. There's ten weeks until the wedding. If you want, we can meet on Monday nights to work on hand-holding techniques." He went to her chair, then took her hand and had her stand. "See? I can do this for you." He pulled out the chair. "And I can seat you, too."

She faced him, looking up to meet his eyes.

His breath caught. He managed, "You'll be wearing heels, right?"

"You're ahead of me."

"Just planning for the height difference. Since we're practicing, maybe we need dress rehearsals." He rested a hand on her shoulder. "You're completely tense, and that makes me awkward. We'll have to work on not loathing one another's touch."

She slipped an arm around his waist. It was not loathsome. They were face to face now, and she said, "Not to mention if we have to dance together."

"Item Five," Declan managed. He had to make the list sound official because she was standing way too close for a game of pretend. "At least three slow dances, and additional dances as desired."

Right now, a fast beat and some distance would have been very desirable, but Rose had no idea what her proximity was doing to him. She rested her hands on his hips. "I'm not sure I've ever slow danced with a guy as tall as you."

"That's why I mentioned heels." He reeled at her touch. "It'll make it easier."

"Dancing backward in heels...makes it easier?" She snickered. "Think about every formal you've ever been to. Once the dancing starts, the shoes come off."

It was hard not to think about other things coming off. "At least for the slow dances?" Maybe this wasn't a great idea. She was using him. He was using her too, sure, but she had a barrier around her heart as well as the conviction that she was simply a better person than everyone she interacted with. Little chance she'd fall for a home-heating tech, even if he could play piano. He on the other hand had to deal with her amazing eyes, her poise, the way she moved, and her electrifying touch.

As with so much in his day job, he'd just have to double-check his grounding and make sure nothing was hot before he touched it.

She had no such compunctions as she pivoted to stand side-by-side with him. "There, that works." Arm around his waist, she tucked up against him. He wrapped an arm around her shoulder and rested his hand on her forearm. Dear heaven, she fit perfectly. Then she stepped back and looked him up and down.

Appraising him. Sure. She fit perfectly, but that didn't make him perfect for her. She said, "Item Six. We hold hands when they're watching us. Arm around my shoulder at the table if they're looking. My arm through yours if we're walking together." She linked arms with him, her fingers resting on his forearm.

If they did this for an entire three-hour reception, Declan was going to lose his mind. Still, there she'd pay attention to her bandmates. It wouldn't be him and her alone at a table, him tantalized by all her attractions and she cataloging all his flaws.

Back around in front of him, she put her arms up to his neck, and he pulled her waist up close. Holding the length of her against him felt awesome, and Declan's resolve quivered like a pine bough in the wind. "We'll manage a slow dance or three. Even without the heels."

She regarded him with mischievous eyes. "Item Six A: at some point during the reception, one kiss."

Declan tensed. "We won't practice that."

It slipped out because she was close enough that he could have. He could have bent and met her lips with his, closed his eyes, and let the world swirl away in warmth and delusion.

This was a performance. Nothing more. Rose was slumming to strike back at her cheating ex and her ex's affair partner. Declan was renting himself out to avenge his sister on her bully.

Startled, Rose stepped backward. "Yeah, we can probably figure that out when the time comes."

Declan retreated to his own chair, his brain abuzz with suggestions that they practice several different styles of kiss. That was the unsolvable problem: Rose had no regard for him. Kissing her would overwhelm him in the moment and leave him feeling stupid afterward.

Some guys were easygoing about differentiating "kisses without feelings" and "kisses with feelings," but for Declan it had to be both. If he kissed her, he'd want *her*. If he ever wanted her, he'd get his heart broken because she'd never want him. She'd established her self-superiority back when he was sixteen, and he'd voiced his disinterest right after. She'd been clear yesterday that she wanted nothing to do with him emotionally, and today they were still being clear.

This was a planning meeting, nothing more. Declan fought to get his head back into the logistics. "Any idea what the reception will be like? Black tie? White tie?"

"We don't even get the fun of dressing up. It's an outdoor buffet with dancing." She left the table momentarily and returned with the invite. "Evening wedding, of course. It's mid-May, so it knocks out one Saturday night, but at least it doesn't destroy Memorial Day weekend."

"Kind of ridiculous that they didn't have the wedding in April, before we all started getting weekend gigs again." Declan shrugged. "Not that I expect either of them to ever think of anyone other than themselves."

Rose sounded hurt. "Travis wasn't always like that."

"Travis was exactly like that or he wouldn't have cheated on you." Declan checked the invitation for the date and time to plug into his phone calendar. "The wedding starts at five, so I'll pick you up at four thirty?"

He looked up to find Rose with large eyes and a distressed frown. "That's not fair to him."

"Are you implying Travis *was* thinking of you when he decided to cheat? I'd have thought someone considerate would have done you the dignity of breaking up before onboarding a new romance."

Rose looked devastated. "Maybe I was just a lousy girlfriend."

Declan's breath caught. Rose must have been hurt, so hurt. His sister had never shown that kind of pain when Mia had been tormenting her. Declan said, "In which case, Travis still should have broken up with you first. He wanted the thrill of having both. You for your loyalty, and Mia for the excitement of deceiving everyone around him. What a rebel rock star, unconstrained by any of society's normal rules."

Rose smirked. "Now you're describing Corwin."

Declan said, "Corwin wouldn't cheat."

She shook her head. "I'm sorry. I'm not usually upset

about Travis. It was a gut-punch when it happened. I found evidence that he was cheating, and he said he wasn't, but he said I wasn't making him happy enough. Two months later, I found more evidence that while I'd been working to make Travis happy, he'd never stopped seeing Mia."

Declan said, "Which also isn't the hallmark of a considerate person."

"It doesn't matter. We're attending a party to witness a contract-signing between two untrustworthy individuals." Rose forced herself to meet Declan's eyes, and again warmth surged through him. She'd been emotionally impaled by these two, but she was keeping it together. "Add Item Eight to the agenda: you have to bring a handkerchief and a throat lozenge. You know, to make it look like I have a terrible cough when the minister talks about true love, and I start to gag."

CHAPTER FIVE

Declan always closed his eyes as he played Lennie Tristano's "Yesterdays." He loved to let the melody flood through him, to play through the asymmetrical rhythms and the augmented eighth notes while the harmonies mingled with the disharmonies. The baby grand beneath his fingers responded with eagerness to sing.

Declan felt through this one with his ears and his heart, sensing not just the piano but the audience. Thursday nights at the Gilbert Ridge Bistro were all his from six to eight o'clock, after which they had an open mic until midnight (or until the bar cleared out).

Declan lived for these nights. The setting was casual, and so were the clothes. The expectations were high, but the terms clear. He'd learned to read the room for the guests' cues. (Not to mention how good he'd gotten at sight-reading sheet music!)

The key was handing the patrons what they wanted.

Some nights they wanted relaxing piano, and other nights they wanted uplifting, and other times they wanted it loud and hard. Declan had endured a rough couple of weeks at first, despairing that his best performances of his best songs were wasted on an audience that didn't want to hear them. Frustrated, Declan had called his music mentor, his first teacher and his guidepost in life: Robert Castleton.

It hurt to think of Bob now. As co-owner of the music school, Bob Castleton had taught most of the area musicians, but he was more than a role model. He'd been like a lighthouse, but last February he'd effectively vanished. Illness, the family said. He'd stopped teaching, handing his students to his oldest daughter and then stepping down from his string quartet. The rumor mill said it wasn't cancer, but the rumor mill couldn't say what it really was.

When Declan had begged for help back then, Bob and his wife Susan had attended the next Thursday night performance. Bob offered pointers about the real-time task of reading the room to select your playlist. Susan coached Declan on how to bond with your audience, giving listeners what they didn't even know they wanted. Bob had returned for the next two weeks until Declan had his wings, and then Bob had backed off so Declan could fly.

Nowadays, regulars came to the bistro specifically to hear Declan. When he recorded an album, some of them bought it. He got paid, and he also got tipped. He did requests. Afterward, he stuck around.

"Yesterdays" was Declan's last song for the evening. From behind, he detected the sounds of random musicians preparing to play once his set ended, and he registered the movement of the audience changing over. His jazz-loving listeners were paying their checks and gathering their coats. The open mic listeners—the ones who loved a good musical experiment—were hanging out at the bar, waiting on the soon-to-be-empty tables.

His piano thrummed out the stormy chords of the finale beneath his fingers, and Declan played the keys as though soothing a nervous animal. Everything was about the pressure and the rhythm and the sound, and then he gathered all the song's themes together to ease them to a close.

The audience applauded. He'd improvised enough to finish at the stroke of eight. That had been another painful lesson: end at seven fifty-eight and customers complained; end at eight-oh-two and his fellow musicians complained.

The restaurant manager took the mic and thanked Declan, then thanked everyone for their patience while the bistro set up for the open-mic portion of the evening.

"Declan!" Sean called, and Declan headed to the corner where Sean was hanging out with a few friends. "Nice work, although you put everyone to sleep."

"You'll just have to wake them up again." Declan nodded toward Sean's guitar case. It looked like he'd brought the steel-stringed acoustic rather than the Super Strat. "Are you playing tonight?"

The open mic nights were laid back. A lot of local musicians showed up with their instruments, but they didn't always know who would play, or what, until it happened. Sometimes Declan stayed for the whole thing. Sometimes he asked for a slot and played a piece the dinner crowd wouldn't have appreciated.

Sean said, "Remember that song I messed around with last week? It's ready to try out in front of an audience."

Declan nodded. "The acoustic ballad? That one's awesome."

"Yeah, but the second Corwin hears it, he's going to say it needs a drum solo and a high-distortion line on the bass." Sean shrugged. "If it works tonight, I'll give it to my brother."

The first act went on, a trio of high schoolers with a twelve-string guitar, a fiddle, a hammer dulcimer, and a distinct folk-rock feel. Sean and his friends grabbed a table, and Declan joined them. "Just water," he told the waitress, but she already had a glass because he did this every week: after his set, he was exhausted and thirsty.

Sean glanced over Declan's shoulder, and then Declan heard, "Hey, guys," followed by the scrape of a chair.

Travis. Declan turned. "Glad you could make it," he said, as though meeting Travis were in any way a planned thing. "Are you playing tonight?"

"Maybe in a bit. Was that 'Lush Life' you ended with?"

Declan said, "Lenny Tristano's 'Yesterdays.'"

Sean stretched. "I've got an acoustic piece to try on a live audience."

Travis raised his eyebrows. "I won't tell Corwin."

Sean shrugged. "I'll tell him myself. Corwin doesn't have the keys to my soul. If I say the piece would sound like garbage as alternative rock, what's he going to do?"

Travis said, "He still writes most of your songs? And Rose still writes the lyrics?"

Declan hadn't realized Rose was Clear Enigma's lyricist. Then again, he'd never paid attention to Clear Enigma. He sometimes listened to alternative or metal (or alternative metal), but he'd never enjoyed playing it. It was hard to dredge up that much anger and keep it burning through a whole performance.

Travis's new group had started in the same vein, but the Tasers drifted toward punk, another genre not in Declan's wheelhouse.

Sean said, "Corwin roughs them out, but Rose makes them spark."

Before Travis could ask more about Rose, Declan gestured to the group on stage. "They're not bad."

Travis rolled his eyes. "Not terrible for a bunch of high schoolers. The girl could use some voice lessons."

Sean said, "I've seen her at the school. She's taking guitar with Edwards."

Travis said, "Like I said, she could use some voice lessons."

Declan didn't ask if Mia had taken voice lessons before Travis tried to shoehorn her into Clear Enigma.

Travis turned to Declan, eyes narrow. "I hear you and Rose are a thing."

Sean snickered. "They're so cute together. It's the height difference."

Travis kept his gaze level. "Watch yourself with her."

Declan recoiled. "Excuse me?"

Robert Castleton had taught him that response. When someone says something offensive, hand him a shovel and let him dig the hole deeper.

Travis had never been one of Bob's best students. "I don't think you know what you're in for with her."

Declan replaced the verbal shovel with a jackhammer. "Do tell."

"She broke up with me a while back, but I still feel protective of her." Sure. Of course. "What she says is not always what she wants. She could make problems."

This was beyond rich. Fortunately, Declan recognized this game because his mother played it when she divorced his father. The game had one rule: *When you can't control the person, control what everyone else thinks about the person.*

Travis said, "I loved her, but I couldn't trust her. Even so, I don't want to see her get hurt."

Declan tilted his head. "You have an odd way of showing it."

Travis's eyes narrowed. "Because I'm warning you?"

"Because of the note you stuck on her wedding invitation, suggesting that if her lonely heart didn't have a plus-one, she could take her second cousin or something."

Travis started. "I didn't write that."

The denial might even have been genuine, but that wasn't Declan's job to figure out. "Also, clarify something. I thought she broke up with you because you were already together with Mia."

Travis shook his head. "See what I mean? Rose isn't trustworthy. I started things with Mia afterward."

"We've got a difference of opinion then, but I don't really care. You're marrying Mia, so Rose isn't your responsibility. She's a strong woman. If I treat her badly, she'll break up with me the same way she broke up with you."

Travis gestured around. "Why isn't she here tonight? If she's not listening to your performances, how serious can she be?"

Tactical error, there. Declan said, "Is Mia here?"

Travis nodded. "She will be in about ten minutes, but you already finished your set. It's odd that Rose wouldn't come to hear you perform. In fact, I don't think she's ever come on a Thursday."

Why would Travis keep track of Rose's whereabouts? "She's busy Thursdays."

Travis smirked. "Busy doing what?"

Declan narrowed his eyes. "Every Thursday night, she has zero accountability to you. Which is the same thing she has every other hour of the week."

Travis ran a hand through his hair. "Look, I'm not telling you how to live." Other than telling Declan how to live, that was. "Just trying to give you some advice."

Declan turned away. "Heard and answered."

A minute later, Travis left.

Declan pulled out his phone and texted Rose. "We need to re-strategize."

CHAPTER SIX

"I hate him." Rose climbed into Declan's Jeep and slammed the door harder than she intended. "I'd gotten to a place where I didn't ever think about Travis, and now he pulls something like that on me."

Was it possible to hear your own blood pressure? Could she get so upset that her heart exploded? She didn't want to find out.

Declan adjusted the heater while pulling onto the main road. "I'm sorry I stirred up bad feelings. I just thought you needed to know what he was saying."

Rose wanted to scream. How many people had Travis lied about her to? Had he interfered whenever she'd looked ready to start a new relationship? Were there a hundred musicians in Maine who'd been about to approach her, only Travis convinced them she was a malignant harpy with a collection of men's still-beating hearts in jars under her sink?

The Jeep was warm, and Rose tried to relax as Declan navigated the paved cow-paths that made up the roads on Hartwell's outskirts. The town center had plenty of right angles, but away from there it was all twists and hills. Walk a quarter mile without paying attention and you could lose yourself.

She huffed. "I can't believe he acted hurt. He only made me do the actual breaking up so he'd seem like the wounded party."

Declan shrugged. "You don't have to convince me. I called him out on that."

She grumbled, "I just want you to get mad at him."

"I did get mad at him. And now we're getting even. Action Item Nine is that we appear in public on a regular basis so our supposed relationship appears real."

"You're so stinking calm." Rose folded her arms. "And why are we doing *this*?"

"Because it's a good thing to do? Because people will see us together outdoors? Because I need to justify the cash I dropped on a metal detector?" Declan gave an uncomfortable laugh. "Work with me here."

Rose flexed her fingers in her gloves. "I'll work with you, but why did you buy a metal detector in the first place?"

"Now that I can answer." He turned up Main Street and headed toward the park. "I've done amateur metal-detecting since I was twelve. One of my uncles took me on a camping trip with my cousins, and we went hiking. I twisted my ankle the first day because I was a klutz, so the family in the next campsite said I could stay with them. My uncle took my cousins back up the mountain, and the other family brought me and all this equipment to a field that used to be a house and a barn. They showed me how to use a metal detector and then how to dig up whatever we found. I found a couple of coins and a nail."

Rose said, "Savage."

"Not at all. It was junk, but it was wicked fun." Declan turned to her. "I got to see the secrets the earth was keeping. I could use a shovel and a sod cutter and dig up history. For my birthday, I asked for a metal detector of my own. I dug up our whole back yard, and then my uncle's back yard, and then the park until the cops stopped me."

Rose sat up. "Wait, I remember this. Didn't you dig a hole out at the music school?"

"Yeah. Susan Castleton wasn't too pleased about that, but I gave Bob everything I found that day." Declan hunched away from her, as though embarrassed. "Good thing you're not in a metal band, or you'd be setting off the detector all day."

Rose murmured, "We also don't have a stud finder."

Declan burst out laughing, and she said, "Wait, um—"

"No, I deserved that." He raised his eyebrows, and now he looked simultaneously unnerved and cute. "Look, everyone needs a weird hobby, and this is mine."

She raised her hands. "No judgment here! Besides, we'd classify as alternative metal if it still existed."

"And it's useful," Declan continued as though she hadn't just said she wasn't passing judgment on the things that made his heart happy. "When someone posts on the Hartwell Public Forum that they lost their wedding ring at the town park soccer fields, I can hunt for it."

In the crowded lot, he handed one metal detector to Rose and kept a larger one for himself. Rose's looked like what would happen if a golf club had a child with a tennis racket, and Declan showed her how to hold it, how to start it, and how to sweep with it. He tossed a penny on the ground so she could sweep the ground to "find" it, and now she too was ready to discover the secrets the earth was keeping.

At the closest soccer field, a smattering of parents huddled on canvas chairs. Girls around seven years old ran after a ball while the coach called to them, "Mark up, team! Get out of the middle!"

Declan approached one of the moms. "I'm on a mission to find a missing wedding ring. How much time is left in the game? And is this Field B?"

"You need us to move?" the mom said, getting up from her chair.

"Metal detectors!" One of the dads approached. "I saw your comment on Hartwell Public Forum. Awesome that you can do this."

Declan shook his head. "Just a chance to get out and make myself useful."

The mom said, "This is Field B, but they have about twenty minutes left, so if you want us to move, we can do that."

"Not a big deal." He headed toward the parked cars, but still had his eyes on the game. "Twenty minutes until we can sweep our target location. Oh, nice block! We should check the grass between here and the parking lot in case it got dropped on the way out, but odds are it's right where the parents are sitting."

Rose eyed the side of the field. "Can we cover all that space in ten minutes between games?"

"Sure, especially with two of us. Great hustle!" He whistled as one of the girls took a shot on goal and missed by twenty feet. They weren't exactly Olympians, but Hartwell wasn't exactly Olympus. The girls wore their uniform shorts over leggings, but at least they couldn't see their breath. March was way too early for soccer matches.

Rose and Declan covered the ground between the parking lot and the field. "The ring won't be deep because it got lost yesterday. If it's in the dirt, it's been stepped on but not buried. Anything far enough below the surface that we can't just pry it out isn't going to be this guy's wedding ring." Declan's detector toned, and he showed her how to scrape over the dirt with the flat side of his trowel. "If we were digging, we'd do this differently, but as I learned when I was an overly enthusiastic twelve-year-old, no one's allowed to dig in the town park."

Rose said, "Why did the guy have his wedding ring off in the first place?"

He stood back up. "See, he failed to post his entire private life on the forum."

Rose said, "We may be helping a cheater."

"While true," Declan said, paying close attention to his sweep pattern, "I can't imagine a Saturday afternoon youth soccer match is the most secretive place to canoodle with one's affair partner."

"I can't imagine that you just said the word *canoodle*. Oh, hey." Her detector lit up, and Declan watched as she inspected the ground. "Ten cents, dude! I'm rich."

She handed him the dime, and he backed off. "Those are your spoils of war, not mine."

She slipped it into her pocket. "If I find another ten thousand of these, I can afford my own metal detector."

"Not nearly that many." He huffed. "It's annoying how many awesome things must be underground here, but we can't dig them out. Oh, hang on." He stopped to shift some gravel, but nothing. "I really hope the ring is at the field. If it's in the parking lot with so many cars, we're not going to be able to find it at all."

"Unless we come back at midnight."

"Yeah, and then Hartwell's Finest will want to know what these two suspicious creatures are doing after dark."

Rose offered, "At least we both own black clothing for performances."

"You in black jeans and a leather jacket, and me in my tuxedo, the pair of us wielding long-handled contraptions in a parking lot by the light of the moon. I'm going with a hard no."

They returned to the field where Declan cheered for both sides. "So close!" "Whoa!" "Yeah, take the shot!"

Rose watched the parents from the corner of her eye, but no one was laughing at them. "Do you know any of the kids?"

He hesitated. "What? No. Why?"

"Any sport is just as good as any other sport as far as you're concerned?" She tucked an arm through his. "It's neat that you're being supportive."

"A game's a game," he said, as though he and she weren't playing a massive game against Travis and Mia.

"Whoa, look at that kick!" Somehow the ball got past the goalie, and he whooped.

He was so loud. She said, "What does it mean, 'Mark up'?"

"It means to cover the person you're supposed to be defending, that way you block anyone passing to them. Ooh, that's going to hurt." One of the girls had taken a shot to the leg, but she waved off the coach and kept playing.

Soccer must be a good dry-run for real life when your boyfriend's phone lit up with a text from the woman he promised he wasn't cheating with. *"I can't wait to see what you have planned for tonight."* You can't call time-out on your life. You have to wave everyone off, pain radiating from the blow, and keep playing your role.

Five minutes later, the parents were picking up their chairs while new parents gathered for the next game. "Now," Declan said, and they swept through the seating area, him closer to the field and her further back. Before the parental eyes of all four teams, Rose discovered the pull-tab from a soda can and a penny. Declan uncovered a small metal car and handed it to the younger sibling of one of the players.

In a way it was like doing scales, making sure you covered everything. It was also like performing—or rather, it was exactly like performing because Rose was so aware of what they expected to see from her, and how well she was giving it to them. The motion. The way she flanked Declan. The excitement from the parents who were rooting for them to strike literal gold.

Declan said, "Not laughing about my metal detectors now, are you?"

Also, it was similar to improv. "No laughter whatsoever, sir. These X-ray vision machines turned me into a superhero."

The parents chuckled. Rose and Declan might not find the ring, but they'd leave 'em with a smile.

"Oh!" Her indicator lit up, and she crouched. Her fingers

ran through the dirt beneath the grass...bumped over something pressed into the ground...was it...? She scraped her fingernails across it—and something came loose, something smooth and cool that looped around her fingertip.

"Ta-dah!" She leaped to her feet holding the wedding ring in the air. Then came a sound she hadn't expected—applause.

She turned by reflex and bowed, and Declan laid his hands on her waist as she came back up. From behind her, he wrapped his fingers around her wrist and raised her ring-bearing hand in the air. "I present to you, ladies and gentlemen, Hartwell's next best metal detector!"

She turned to him, and suddenly they were looking right in one another's eyes. He was triumphant, and she flushed without averting her gaze.

It was a performance. They were giving the bystanders a show.

Declan said, "Do you think I can take you on a real metal detecting expedition now?"

She got on one knee and slipped the ring onto his pinky finger. "I do."

The bystanders cheered, and she sprang back up on tiptoes to give Declan a hug. He looked super surprised, and then she thrilled all over as he hugged her in return.

As Declan drove the spaghetti-like road to the music school, Rose wondered about all the times the metal detector had pinged off something underground, something she couldn't see and wasn't allowed to excavate.

When she glanced at Declan, her heart pinged as well.

"It's always the best feeling when you return something to someone." Declan watched the curving road, not his passenger, so Rose could enjoy his smile as much as she wanted. "I found someone's keys at a beach. I happened to be there with the newer metal detector when they asked for help. They tried to pay me because it would have cost fifty bucks to make a new key, but I told them to donate it instead because I'd gotten what I wanted: a chance to test my equipment."

Rose said, "Who usually goes with you?"

Declan shrugged. "No one."

"You have two metal detectors."

"My old detector didn't have some of the better features, but I didn't want to get rid of it."

Rose teased, "So I got the lousy one? And I found the ring anyhow?"

Declan frowned. "Don't say it like that. My first one is easier to use and less likely to ping off something buried ten feet down."

"I'm just teasing. I wouldn't use the better one regardless because I'd probably break it."

Declan said, "Have you ever broken a keyboard?"

She exclaimed, "I plead the fifth," and he laughed. "It's unfair. No one minds that Beethoven destroyed pianos."

Declan snorted. "No one minds *now*. I'm sure they minded at the time."

Rose gave a dramatic sigh. "That's the reward for greatness. Everyone sees what you became, so they stop harping on about all the priceless things you shattered when you were young and stupid."

Declan parked at the music school. The owner of the wedding ring would meet them here to pick it up, and Rose would go to practice with Clear Enigma.

As she pulled on her backpack, Rose said, "Now we'll get to see what a cheater looks like. Do you think he'll look smug?"

Declan raised his eyebrows. "Maybe he'll trudge in humiliated, with his angry wife and livid mistress flanking him on either side."

"Perfect." Rose checked her messages as they entered

the foyer, but none of her group had arrived yet. Declan went for the piano in the waiting area, just an upright, but guaranteed to be in tune. "Do I get a concert?"

"Travis sounded horrified that you weren't listening at Gilbert Ridge, so I'm rectifying that." Declan raised the keyboard cover.

He launched into Mozart's "Rondo Alla Turca". Rose watched over his shoulders as his fingers flew over the keyboard. This piece wasn't about intonation as much as rhythm and accuracy, and she let the song flow through her. Just as she was getting into it, though, he switched to a tune she didn't recognize.

She leaned against his shoulders. "Do I get a medley of Declan's Greatest Hits?"

He nodded. "Yes, in my musical greatness, I wrote them all." He slid into Alicia Keyes' "A Thousand Miles," this time really leaning into the intonation, and she stepped away to watch from alongside.

In her area of music, Rose had gotten used to guitar players with their faces contorted as they concentrated on a riff. In alternative, you had to look angsty. One of their fans had taken Clear Enigma's photos from a December gig and photoshopped giant insects into their hands, which worked like magic because their expressions worked great for someone grasping the bristly leg of a wasp.

By contrast, Declan smiled. He was enjoying himself even as he was letting his fingers wander from one song into the next. This wasn't a performance as much as what happened naturally when you left a pianist alone in a room with a piano.

He changed things up, and now he was playing one of Bach's two part inventions. She laughed, and suddenly he was syncopating Bach while breathing a dusky-smooth air into the keys. It was Bach, and it was jazz. It was amazing.

She grinned. "You had me there. I didn't know you could do that."

"Susan made me practice these all the time. I got bored."

"Me too, but I found other things to play rather than

find different ways of playing the same thing." She studied Declan's fingers. Although she'd started on piano, she'd shifted to keyboard when she decided to focus on rock rather than classical or jazz. Despite the obvious similarity, the techniques were different.

Now Declan focused a bit harder, and jazzy Bach veered straight into country.

Rose laid her hand over her heart in mock horror. "Hillbilly Bach!"

"I have sinned. Some lines shouldn't be crossed." Declan changed styles again, this time slowing it way down so it reverberated like a love ballad. "Does this make your teeth hurt less?"

"Hush." She sat on the piano bench, and he slid over while she set her hands on the keys. "I wish I still had the sheet music for the original." She picked through the notes while her fingers remembered the muscle movements, and once she had it back, he stopped playing on the right side of the keyboard while she ground it out on the lower left-hand notes, as if Sean were growling into a mic about the demise of a love affair.

Declan exclaimed, "Bach, no!" but she leaned hard into the bass and worked the pedals, then slowed the tempo until what should have been a warm-up exercise thundered with unsettled rage.

"Savage!" Corwin flew down the stairs. "I come out of the worst meeting of my life only to hear you torturing poor Johann Sebastian. I love it!" He folded his arms and leaned against the wall. "Do that again and I may beg you to write some lyrics just to make the poor man rise from the dead to kick my butt."

"Couldn't happen soon enough." Two black-haired women followed him down the stairs from the third floor offices. The speaker was Corwin's oldest sister, Lindsey. Alongside her was Sierra, their middle sister and also Rose's apartment-mate. "Someone ought to."

"It'll be better than you beating me with the stick up your back." Corwin didn't look good, and beside him,

Lindsey and Sierra both looked wrecked. All three Castleton siblings, having a meeting? Was it about their father?

The three together were clearly a set, although not interchangeable. Lindsey was tall and strong, whereas Sierra was shorter and had soft edges at odds with Corwin's sharpness.

Corwin added, "If there's a zombie apocalypse, starting with Bach is a classy way to go."

Declan stood from the piano bench. "Hey, Linz, Sierra. I didn't realize you'd be here."

Lindsey side-eyed her brother. "Family meeting."

Declan said, "About your father? How is he?"

Rose had been struggling for a way to ask that, and Declan had just come out with it.

"Yes, it's about our father. Criminy." Corwin rolled his eyes. "The news went from bad to worse, okay? He's not going to recover, and everything is sliding downhill faster than a skateboard off Mount Washington, and Lindsey wants to script how all the housework gets taken care of, as though the worst thing we have to figure out is how to shovel Mom and Dad's driveway." Corwin pulled the practice room keys from his pocket. "I'll clean the gutters every fall so Mom doesn't have to, and that will prolong Dad's life. Thanks, Lindsey, for saving the whole lousy world."

Corwin stomped down the steps to the practice rooms while Rose looked back and forth.

Eyes round, Sierra turned to Rose. "I'm sorry. He shouldn't have dragged you into that."

Lindsey muttered, "So sorry for looking out for *our mother.*"

Sierra ran her fingers through her short hair. "He's grieving."

"The Grief Society of Maine will have to photograph him as the face of their next sympathy campaign." Lindsey shoved her hands in her pockets. "Whatever. He agreed to help. That's all we needed." And then Lindsey went out the front door.

Sierra glanced at Declan where he stood alongside the piano bench. "I assume Rose is here for practice, but what about you?"

Rose shivered. "Oh, this is a story."

Sierra brightened. "I'd love a story. It's got to be better than brainstorming ways to keep Mom from needing to sell our home."

How to explain this in such a way that Sierra didn't immediately try to dissuade them? Sierra would doubtless murmur, "Love is too important to make it a lie."

Instead, Declan opted for a different, also-true story. "Rose and I searched the soccer fields this morning to find a lost wedding ring. The owner is going to meet us here."

Sierra beamed. "Oh, how sweet! She must have been heartbroken!"

Declan produced the ring from his wallet. "*He.*"

Sierra scolded, "Don't store a wedding ring with your money."

"It was safest in my wallet."

"Love and money don't mix." Sierra held it to the light. "This is well-worn. How did he lose it?"

Cheating, obviously. There aren't a lot of reasons to remove your wedding ring.

Declan took back the ring. "No clue. My job was to find it. Rose and I each took a metal detector and swept the field."

Rose said, "Declan says metal detectors reveal the secrets the earth is keeping," and Sierra clasped her hands at her chest, wide-eyed.

Sean entered the lobby, escorting a man in his mid-thirties. "Declan, you have a visitor."

The man's eyes went right to the ring in Declan's hand. "Oh, thank heaven. I cannot thank you enough for finding that."

Declan handed it over. "Glad to help."

The man pulled a black band off his ring finger, then slipped the gold one into its place. "My wife kept telling me it wasn't the end of the world, but I know it hurt her."

Rose had her eyes glued to the black ring. "But you were already wearing a ring—?"

The guy held it up so she could see its dull rubbery tone. "It's silicone. I'm a mechanic."

"Oh!" Declan turned to Rose. "Have you ever heard of 'degloving'?" When she shook her head, he urged, "Don't look it up. I had to see some awful pictures for my HVAC certification."

The mechanic said, "When I'm at work, I use a silicone band because if these get caught in an engine, they snap right off. If a metal ring gets caught, it'll take your finger… if you're lucky."

Rose gasped at the mental image. "Oh!"

Not cheating. Not cheating at all.

Declan said, "It's something you don't have to consider while playing piano. Most of the guys at my company don't wear anything metal. No wrist watches, no chains—but I hadn't made the connection."

The mechanic shuddered. "Watches are the worst. Hit both ends of a terminal with the band and you're wearing a lifelong map of exactly where it was."

A lifelong map of exactly where the lightning hit: emotional injuries did that too.

Sean looked nauseated. "Silicone's sounding better and better."

"I get flak from the other guys, but whatever. They do what they want, and I'll wear what I want." The mechanic shoved the silicone band into his pocket. "I went to my son's game straight from the shop, and my ring must have come out of my pocket when I texted my wife the score." He shook Declan's hand. "Thank you so much, man."

Declan said, "Actually, Rose is the one who found it."

"With *your* metal detector. You'd have found it just fine without me." But she shook the mechanic's hand as well.

The guy pulled out his wallet and pulled out some cash, but Declan raised his hands. "No need. I'm glad to have helped, plus it gave me a chance to show off my metal detectors."

The guy protested, "You gotta take something."

Declan raised his eyebrows. "How about you bring your wife and kid to the Gilbert Ridge Bistro on a Thursday night and listen to me play? Six to eight o'clock."

"Jazz piano," Rose added. "He's really good."

"Thanks, I will," he said as he left.

Declan hadn't just helped a cheater cover his tracks. Declan had helped a good guy who'd made a thoughtless mistake, and a thoughtless mistake shouldn't have lifelong consequences.

Declan turned to Rose, his eyebrows raised. "Well?"

He looked marginally smug, and embarrassment crept up Rose's throat. She swallowed. "What can I say? I was wrong."

He winked at her, and she flushed. "First time I've ever heard you say that."

CHAPTER SEVEN

Sean sat at the kitchen table, headphones plugged into his multi-effects pedal, whaling away at some tune Declan could barely hear through the Super Strat's metal strings.

Whatever happened at practice after Declan had left—it had been bad. Bad with a capital B. Bad like a B minor 7 chord with the distortion turned all the way up. Sean wouldn't talk about it. He'd blown off the question every way possible until Declan had decided it was too fresh, too awful. Corwin on the stairwell had snapped at his sister and slammed doors on the way to practice, but Corwin during practice must have gone volcanic.

Declan grabbed a soda and retreated.

Rose. She'd been there too.

Declan had no right to ask Rose about the practice. Asking her would be rude beyond belief because she'd think (rightly) that he wanted to pry. Moreover, she might be as upset as Sean. Making her rehash what might have been a contentious afternoon would leave her more upset.

On the other hand, was he justified in asking how she was holding up? He and she weren't together—not really. They were co-performers working on a shared project, and you didn't contact your coworkers after hours because you heard through a friend that something might have happened after you went home for the day.

Although...Declan could see doing something like that. After the fallout from Mia's bullying, his own sister had made a lifelong friend when a high school acquaintance called just to check on how she was.

If Rose was offended by Declan reaching out, she could ignore his text. Or she'd introduce Action Item Ten: *No talking unless we have to.* Either way, it was useful information.

He texted her. "Are you okay? Sean came home from practice looking like five miles of rough road."

Declan played the two-part invention he'd been doing with Rose, not dolling it up this time. Bach had designed these pieces specifically for practice, and they were engaging enough that Declan had to pay attention.

Her reply appeared. "Practice was rough."

He broke off and texted, "Are you okay?"

The status bar indicated she was typing something, but eventually the only thing that appeared was, "Not really."

He hit the button to call her number, and she answered.

"I'm sorry. I didn't mean to sound like I was standing on the edge of a bridge." Her voice was wobbly. "Corwin was like a hurricane, and then I got home and Sierra was just—defeated."

Declan said, "I'm so sorry." He hadn't put it together that since Rose and Sierra were sharing a townhome, Rose was going to get a double dose of whatever had happened to the Castletons. "The whole thing with Bob sounds awful."

"I can't even conceive of it. Sierra sat at the table talking for like an hour, and we kept making tea, and she tried to make me eat cookies because cookies make everything better, only she was too nauseated to eat."

Declan said, "So, this is about more than cleaning gutters?"

"A lot more than cleaning gutters." Long silence. Then, "Corwin griped about the chores because that's something you can do."

Declan said, "I feel that way sometimes. Like, everything else in your life is a mess, but at least if you put gas in the car, you can drive to work tomorrow."

"Yeah, same with vacuuming the living room or washing the dishes. Hey, look, I accomplished something. The thing is—"

Rose broke off.

Declan said, "The thing is, Bob isn't going to get better?"

"No, it's— I didn't understand what they were saying back in February when they said he had frontotemporal dementia. He's in his fifties, right?"

Declan said, "Something like."

"I thought by 'dementia' they meant it would build and Bob would get more forgetful until he was eighty, but this is the early-onset kind...? It's fast. It's already taken a lot of his fine motor coordination, and it's taking his word recall and his emotional control as well. He can't play music anymore."

Declan's heart stopped. Bob's life was music. Bob was a top-notch violinist and a teacher and a mentor. How could he not be able to play music?

"Last week they got a second opinion from a world-renowned specialist in Boston, and it was worse. Lindsey made Corwin and Sierra talk this out because Bob's going to need to continuous care. And soon."

Declan protested, "But Bob's young."

"That's the point. The early-onset stuff hits hard and fast. He's going to die. But not before he loses all his memories and all his coordination and all his emotional regulation. His fine motor control is shot, but Sierra's in tears because they're losing *him*." Rose's voice broke. "His personality is changing. Lindsey says Bob can't stay alone any longer, so when their mother goes to play for the church services or when she's holding rehearsals or when she's teaching, someone's got to stay with him. They had to lock up the car keys, and Corwin pulled the spark plugs out of his car. Bob's judgment is gone."

Declan closed his eyes. "That can't be right. Can't they get another opinion? Some kind of medication to slow it down?"

"The first two opinions already agree. Sierra and I were reading webpages about this stuff, and they agree too. There's no medication. The doctors can give him an antidepressant to keep him calm while he forgets everything and loses his coordination, but they can't even slow it down. On Friday, Lindsey walked into the house to find smoke filling the kitchen. Bob was boiling an empty pot, but he didn't see anything wrong."

Declan closed the keyboard on the piano, then sat with his elbows on the cover, his face in his hands.

Bob. Bob Castleton.

He choked out, "How's Susan taking it? They've been married for…what, thirty years?"

"Susan's a rock, but I don't know how you'd take this well, or if you should." Rose's voice was thready. "Sierra was in pieces, and I don't know how to comfort her. She's trying to be strong for her mom, and—"

Rose broke off.

Declan murmured, "And no one's being strong for you."

"I'm a bystander. I also got to watch Corwin melt down during practice, only he never mentioned his father. Instead he ranted about every single thing wrong with the world, with the music industry, with our competition, with every venue we've ever played. He told me he's glad we're messing with Travis's head and he hopes Mia dies of bitterness and on and on and on."

Declan altered the pitch of his voice, again more soothing. "And no one's being strong for you."

Rose said, "It's not about me."

Declan said, "After you've been strong for everyone else,

it does become about you."

She didn't answer.

Declan moved from the piano to his bed, propping himself on his elbows. "You listened to Corwin. Then you comforted Sierra. What do you do with all that pain afterward?"

Rose muttered, "Well, now I'm dumping it on you."

"That's a good thing if it helps you keep supporting them."

Rose said, "Did Sean rant about it?"

"He won't talk at all."

"Figures. I'm the one who bled all over you."

"I don't mind." If she recalled, he'd asked to hear what was going on. "Bob was important to you too."

"We didn't interact as much as I did with Susan." Susan was the piano and brass instructor, whereas Bob focused on the strings. "He's just been around forever."

That should have been the case for Declan too, then, except—

Rose said, "Except you spent a lot of time with him."

"I did, but— It's complicated. I started piano lessons when my parents got divorced. My mother kept messing with my head, so my dad put me in therapy. The therapist told him to find me some area of competency. I stank at sports, so he enrolled me in Scouts and piano lessons."

Rose said, "Your mom messed with your head?"

"She hates my father. With her, it's all about winning. My stepmother is such a better human being." Declan sighed. "That's my dirty laundry. When I started, I couldn't deal with Susan because whenever she tried to teach me, no matter what she said or how she said it, she was just one more woman saying I was garbage like my dad."

Rose whistled. "You're not garbage!"

"Neither is my dad, but my mom was poisoning my mind. Susan and Bob agreed Bob should take over instead. After two years I did shift back to Susan, but Bob had me under his wing when everything went nuts." Declan rolled onto his back and stared at the ceiling. "Losing him—

losing him so fast... This stinks. He's supposed to be there."

Declan had been taking piano for two months when Bob showed him the soundproof practice rooms in the basement. Bob said, "Next time you need to scream about how unfair it all is, you come here. You scream as much as you want. And when you're screamed-out, you come find me."

Bob and Susan had been the most stable couple Declan knew. When Dad and Mari had decided to get married, it had been Bob that Declan ranted to. It had been Bob and Susan together who finagled the billing to keep Declan enrolled after his jealous mother refused to shell out even one more cent for lessons.

Declan laid it out for Rose. He talked, and she sighed, and she agreed, and she asked questions. "I didn't realize," she said at one point. "You always had everything so together."

"It's why I've got the job I have." Declan blew out a breath. "My mother agreed to pay half for college, and when the first tuition bill came due, she refused. It would all have been on my father, but my sister had transferred to a private school after everything with Mia, and then Kimi would also have college tuition. We couldn't afford it all."

Rose sounded puzzled. "Why would your mother have paid for your sister's tuition but not yours?"

"Oh, Kimi's actually my stepsister. I consider her my real sister."

Rose sounded surprised. "That's really cool how your father and stepmother became your real family." Rose paused. "And of course, she's *really* your sister because now you're doing all this to settle the score for her with Mia."

Declan cut himself off before he could reply. *Doing all this.*

Calling Rose and talking to her...taking Rose metal-detecting... "All this" wasn't that much, was it? Declan hadn't even needed to call Rose tonight, except it had felt right.

Except for Rose, talking to Declan was *work*. He'd offered support, and instead he was dumping his grief about Bob and Susan into her lap the same way Sierra had done and Corwin had tried not to do.

Rose had stepped right into the role of looking out for him. She considered herself better than him. She always had. Now she was looking at his parents' divorce as another way he was her inferior, not to mention his education and profession.

He'd just wrap this up as fast as possible. "Anyhow, at that point I de-enrolled from college. I'd done the high school specialization in HVAC, so I applied for full time work at the place where I'd done my co-op. Now here I am. No college debt, and a really good job."

Rose chuckled. "I'll say. Up here, you're always going to have work in the winters."

Declan closed his eyes. "Yeah, it's the opposite of most musicians, where they work the whole summer, and then once the tourists go home..."

"Poof!" Then Rose changed tone. "Corwin had wanted us to get gigs in Florida over Christmas and spring break, but now he doesn't want to. Because of his dad."

"I get that. Family's the most important thing." Declan ought to set Rose free, since she viewed the conversation as billable hours for which she wasn't billing. "Well, I just wanted to see if you were okay. I'll let you go."

"Oh. Um, okay." She hesitated. "Given what Travis said to you, I should stop by the Gilbert Ridge on Thursday."

In public, she'd get some benefit from the pretense. Declan tried to sound cheerful. "See you then! If you have any requests, let me know." And with that, Declan got off the phone so Rose could return to her real life.

CHAPTER EIGHT

While Rose sat with her back to the bar in Gilbert Ridge, Declan played Beethoven's piano sonata #8 in C minor, aka "Pathétique."

He couldn't see her from the piano bench, although after he'd ended his previous piece (a jazz work that might have been his own composition) he'd scanned the dining room. Looking for her? Or was he looking for Travis and Mia so he could figure out whether he needed to seem in love?

Now he was back to playing, and it was like Rose had said before—he wasn't there. His consciousness inhabited that piano as if it were another limb with its own nerve endings. Transported to a world of his own creation, Declan was breathtaking.

He'd have been breathtaking anyhow. She'd never come to the bistro ahead of the open mic nights. Declan had dressed for the casual atmosphere, wearing tan pants and a blazer. Someday she'd like to see him perform at a wedding. He must look astounding in a tux.

Speaking of weddings, this was a lot of work just to wipe the smug grins off the faces of two cheaters.

On the phone this Sunday, with no need to perform, Declan had sounded sympathetic. Unless he were holding that conversation right in front of Travis, why would he have been pretending? She'd begun believing he cared until the moment he noticed he'd punched his time clock and his shift was over, at which point he'd hustled Rose off the line. They weren't together; they just happened to have the same destination.

Mia sidled up to Rose. "I'd been wondering if you'd ever come to hear your beloved at work."

Speaking of "not being there," Rose had been watching Declan too intently to keep an eye out for intruders. Doubtless Travis was watching the interaction from outside her peripheral vision. "I hear him quite a bit, but tonight he's playing that for me."

Mia snickered. "Remember in high school, we'd call that 'Pathetic'?"

Oh, look, you dropped your mean-girl comment right there on the floor. Rose leaned her elbows against the bar and kept her eyes riveted to Declan. "We said and did a lot of stupid things in high school."

"Speak for yourself." Mia folded her arms as she too watched Declan. Declan, looking passionate as he stroked that piano and evoked the most amazing sounds from its gleaming body. He wasn't emotional when he talked, but when he played, it went right through Rose.

Although come to think about it, he'd been very emotional when he talked about Bob. Talked about his parents' divorce. Asked about Rose's own emotions.

Mia said, "Is Corwin thrilled now that you're the famous Rosalind Ward?"

Rose's brow furrowed. "I've become famous?"

Mia huffed. "Finding that man's wedding ring?"

Rose started. "Who even knows about it?" For that matter, how did Mia know about it?

Mia said, "Do you live under a rock?"

"I live in Hartwell." Rose rolled her eyes. "Isn't that kind of the same?"

Mia sniffed. "You walked past a whole stack of the *Hartwell Herald* and didn't even look?"

Rose never looked at the free twelve-page weekly scandal sheet that served almost entirely as a vehicle for local ads, its existence justified by the occasional breathless bit of information. The *Herald* ran groundbreaking pieces like, "Aldermen vote on repainting lines in the town hall parking lot," where the headline was more newsy than the rest of the article. Stacks of them got dumped the grocery store and restaurants to grab on the way out. The *Herald* was handy for starting a draft in the chimney.

Rose huffed. "That's exactly my point about Hartwell, if finding a ring at a soccer field makes it into the paper."

Mia poked around on her phone, so Rose's gaze returned to Declan. Energy coursed over his body as he began the third movement. Beethoven was in top form in this piece, but Declan was emoting through the strings and the keys to make it feel as though Rose had never heard these notes before.

Mia shoved her phone at Rose. "See? It's on their website too."

Rose expanded the picture to find herself holding the ring in the air, and Declan with his arm around her shoulders.

Well, this ought to convince Mia they were legit. Rose and Declan could stop performing right this instant because Mia would never question it again.

Mia tried to take back the phone, but Rose said, "Can I read?" There it was in the text: auto mechanic loses his wedding ring, so a local couple dedicates their morning to restoring the symbol of love to his grieving ring finger.

And I thought I was hyping the emotion. Rose scrolled down for the comments because those were always a delight, and there she found a second photo: her slipping the ring onto Declan's hand.

How totally perfect in every way. Why was there a reporter at that soccer field? Why hadn't Rose thought to herself, *Enough is perfectly enough*? No, she'd had to shoot for the encore that would crown the rest of the performance and leave the audience thinking about them for days.

At least the mechanic thought the "proposal" was funny. Mia, not so much.

Wearing a beatific smile, Rose passed back Mia's phone. "Isn't Declan amazing? He heard about the missing ring, and there was no possibility that he wasn't going to help."

Mia said, "You aren't ashamed to get caught proposing using someone else's ring?"

Well, you weren't ashamed to be caught using someone else's boyfriend. Rose kept her eyes riveted to Declan. "Did Travis's proposal make the paper?"

Mia took a long breath, and then she said, "I know it was hard for you when Travis and I got together, but I want you to know, I forgive you."

Rose went momentarily blind with outrage. Mia forgave her? For what? For being angry that Travis was two-timing her? For ditching a friend who thought her boyfriend was fair game?

Rose managed to say, "Thank you. I've never doubted your generosity of spirit."

Declan finished up the Pathétique, and Rose joined the applause, making sure her performance was every bit as good as his. When he scanned the dining area, she waved.

When he saw Rose, his face lit up.

Rose beamed back at him—and then came the pain. He'd faked joy to see her, and she'd responded with the real thing.

No, no. The more Rose spent time pretending to be Declan's girlfriend, the more she remembered the emotional rush of being someone's actual girlfriend. When Declan smiled as though he loved her, it brought back how it used to feel when a man loved her for real. Now she was hungering for it to be real.

And that? That led to convincing yourself the bad behaviors were excusable. When you wore rose-colored glasses, all the red flags looked black.

As Declan crossed the room, she longed to run. This was a mistake. She was not his type. To be specific, she was *quintessentially* not his type. She had "Action Items". She had total clarity.

She had a problem.

Declan scooped Rose into his arms. "Oh, I'm so glad you could come."

His guttural "oh" went right through her. Rose pressed against him, cheek to his shoulder, eyes closed. "You were amazing," she murmured.

Mia said, "You really were amazing," her voice higher-pitched than usual. Rose's hair stood on end as Mia touched Declan's arm. "I've always loved the Pathétique, and you were marvelous."

Declan said, "Thank you. Rose asked me to play it just for her."

Rose had done nothing of the sort, but at least their minds ran along the same lines. Plus, she appreciated the zing.

She didn't move from Declan's arms because he felt so good, and that in itself ached. She needed to get a grip. She was on the verge of hurting herself to keep Mia from hurting her. She shouldn't have cared when Mia crowed about how Rose was still single. Mia would have brandished the tin cup she thought was a gold trophy, but at least Rose's would have been an honest pain.

Mia exclaimed, "Oh, look who's here!" She got on tip-toes and waved toward the door, and now Rose stepped back from Declan. As Travis approached, Rose's shoulders tensed.

Declan took her hand, and she clenched hard.

Travis said, "Sorry I'm late."

Rose fought vertigo. "Mia was telling us how much she loves the Pathétique, since Declan played it for me."

Let Travis waste brain cells untangling her sentence. At this point, Mia was irritated enough that she would take offense at anything, so Rose might as well make every word sound like intrigue. *Die mad, my salty former friend.*

Travis said, "Jay's holding a table for us, so we should head over."

Mia turned to Rose. "Before I go, you haven't RSVP'd yet for my bridal shower."

Rose said, "I had no idea I was invited," because that was true. "I didn't get an invitation."

"Maybe it got lost in the mail, but are you coming?"

Rose would rather go to a meat packing plant and jump feet-first into the nearest grinder, but that would have sounded harsh. "When?"

Mia said, "Two weeks from now, on Saturday."

Declan put in, "That's the day we're going hiking."

Bless him. Rose made herself look sad. "I'm so sorry, Mia, but we have plans."

That was to say, *now* she had plans.

Travis said, "Where are you headed?"

Declan said, "A relative is restoring a Revolutionary-War-era property up north, and I've been dying to do some metal detecting on the site."

Rose said with a tight smile, "You know, like we did in the paper." Rose put her hand on Declan's arm. "Mia just told me! The *Herald* got wind of the wedding ring. They even had pictures."

Mia said to Travis, "She got caught proposing with a married man's ring."

Declan said, "Well, at least all four of us know Rose would never mess with someone else's relationship."

As Mia tensed, Travis pivoted her toward his friend's table. With one last look at Declan, Mia followed him.

Declan turned to Rose, but he didn't pull her close. The performance was over. "So...about that metal-detecting trip...?"

Metal-detecting beat meat-grinding, even if being with Declan chewed her heart to bits. "Sounds like a plan. In two weeks, let's uncover some secrets."

CHAPTER NINE

Declan adjusted the straps of his backpack. He could see his breath.

Looking brave as well as cold, Rose had her hands deep in her jacket pockets. "Lead on, sir."

Leaving the Jeep in the dirt where the "road" ended, they began their hike. Declan had a map along with a verbal list of landmarks because only the barest of trails led up the mountainside to the target site. "We're looking for a rock wall," he reminded her.

She sighed. "Did you ever think how every one of those rocks got dug out of the ground? I can't imagine being that desperate for a wall."

Declan chuckled. "Maybe they were desperate for a place to put unwanted rocks."

Unwanted emotions couldn't get stacked the same way, and they were less useful for setting out boundaries. You knew when you crossed a rock wall. You didn't know at first when you crossed an emotional boundary. Like you'd hug a woman to prove to two bystanders how thrilled you were to see her, only surprise! You actually felt thrilled to see her. She'd pretend to be thrilled that you played music for her, only surprise! Your stupid heart responded with pride that you'd made her happy. Except you hadn't made her happy. You were proud over nothing.

Declan had wanted to climb this mountain since January but had been waiting for his cousin to join him. His cousin had been unenthusiastic, to say the least. Declan told himself Rose was a convenient stand-in. She'd use the second metal detector so they could scan twice as much ground, plus a companion mitigated the dangers of hiking an unmarked trail. It excused her from buying a bridal shower gift. This trip was all business.

He'd keep telling himself that.

Breathing hard, they ascended in silence. Periodically Declan checked his map, choosing their path while keeping his ears open for Rose's steps. They were both decked out in sturdy boots, jeans, and multiple layers on top. Those would come off as the hike intensified and the day warmed. Their backpacks were loaded with food and water, gear, and one metal detector each. Rose had insisted Declan carry the better one. "If I fall off the cliff, at least you won't have to replace the expensive equipment."

In return, he'd pouted. "But the cookies are in your backpack."

At the rock wall, they stopped to drink. "About halfway," he offered.

"You'd think they'd put a building further down the mountain." Rose shook her head. "Could you imagine doing this every time you had to visit civilization?"

At nine o'clock they reached the target site. Declan laid out the equipment while Rose studied a squared-off rock foundation. The area looked to have been cleared but then grown over again with thickets, and it was mostly level. A stream ran nearby.

Declan handed her a granola bar. "Before we scan, we'll map out the most likely sites. The house foundation is obvious, but we need to determine where they had outbuildings, privies, the road, the well, their garbage pit, and whether the stream bed changed course."

Rose drew back. "This is not like finding a wedding ring!"

Declan arched his eyebrows. "It is exactly like finding a wedding ring. If you remember, we figured out where the cars would have been parked, where the parents would have been sitting, and what route the ring-bearer would have taken between the two. The only difference is accounting for a three-century gap."

He sketched the site while Rose hunted for anything that seemed like a non-natural formation. She identified what might have been a rock wall. She and he studied the trees and the curves of the land. He located what he thought was an outbuilding's foundation, and from there he found a cluster of lilac bushes that might have been the sites of outhouses or the family graveyard.

She said, "And we're not digging there, right?"

He shrugged. "It's not as gross as it sounds. Everything is long since decomposed, but considering how often people drop their cell phones in the toilet, some belongings would have fallen into the privy. Speaking of which, let me show you how we'll dig."

He scanned inside the foundation until the metal detector pinged. Then Declan cut through the top layer of dirt with a sod knife, peeled back the plant roots, and started digging. He dumped the dirt onto a tarp.

They were shoulder to shoulder, and the Rose detector in Declan's mind kept pinging off her.

Right there. It didn't matter that she was judging him every second they were together. He was having a hard time concentrating on his technique, on listening to the scrape of his trowel against undisturbed dirt, on the delicate process of removing objects that might be artifacts but turned out to be stones. He showed her how the pinpointer could direct their search.

Whatever they were looking for was eight to twelve inches underground, so he let Rose take over. For once let her judge how hard it was, rather than how inadequate he was.

"Odd." Rose huffed. "Black dirt."

"What?" He stuck his hand into the granules she'd cleared from the hole. "That's not dirt. That's ash."

He sat back hard, staring at nothing.

She tilted her head. "We're digging up their fireplace?"

"If we're lucky. Otherwise the house burned down."

She stopped digging. "Are we going to find human bodies? Because I really don't want to find that."

That's one of the risks he'd signed up for when he started looking at the deep past. Voice thin, he said, "Life was rough back then. You never really know what you're going to unbury."

She handed back the trowel. Well, then. Not so perfect after all, are we?

Just beneath the black dirt, Declan changed to a scraping motion. The sound changed. He lay prone and worked with his fingers, and finally his hand emerged holding a long, flat object.

They cleared it off together, and she said, "A fork!"

He worked over the edges with a soft cloth. "Indeed. You have correctly identified a fork."

She nudged him. "I could go to the convenience store and get you a fork."

He said, "Wouldn't be nearly as fun. Well, that's the end of your certification training. I hereby authorize you to search and retrieve on your own."

The ash layer persisted across the entire site, both a good and a bad thing. Whenever he dug through that layer, Declan imagined the devastation of a fire raging through a homestead. The fear. The loss of everything that could keep a family alive in the wilderness. The possible deaths —of people, of animals. Deaths not necessarily from flame or smoke but from exposure afterward. What if it happened during a blizzard when they couldn't get down the mountain to shelter?

Good from an archaeological perspective, though, the same way the tragedy of Pompeii benefitted the study of ancient Rome.

By lunchtime, they'd found two buttons, a coin, and what might have been the base of a lamp. He washed his hands as best he could in the frigid stream, then set their lunch out on the rocks.

Rose shivered violently as she scrubbed off the dirt. "It's really just melted ice," Declan called to her.

By comparison, the sun and hard work had warmed them up. They'd shed their jackets, and Declan considered removing his flannel shirt and working in only a t-shirt. They ate lunch in the sunshine, listening to the breeze shaking tree branches beginning to bud. The stream gurgled over the stones. It was too early in the year for dragonflies or frogs, but Declan watched for fish. On the other side, the bushes rustled as something ran from cover to cover.

"Chipmunks, do you think?" When Rose didn't answer, Declan turned to her. She was gazing out across the stream, face strained. She didn't look sick. More as if she were in pain. "You okay?"

She kept her gaze fixed on the distant rocks. "I shouldn't ask this, but what is your type? Since I'm quintessentially not it."

The stream had been icy, but her words spiked a deeper chill through him.

She finally looked around, and their eyes met.

She realized. She had to have realized.

She glanced away. "Your previous girlfriends don't really — Well, I don't see the pattern."

Or rather, she had seen the pattern, and she realized she fit right into it. Smart women with a quick wit and a warm smile. Women who loved music and valued family.

In the continuing silence, broken only by the stream over smooth rock, she put her empty sandwich wrapper into her backpack. Out came the bag of cookies. "I made these last night."

"Thanks." Declan didn't reach for one. "It's not about your type. I said that because I was angry at you."

Her brow contracted. "How did I make you angry? We barely even talked."

"But when you talked about me, think about that. Right after the statewide music competition where you beat me by one point. You bragged to my friends about how you trashed me and kept me out of the final round."

She sat up, wide-eyed.

He glared away. "I heard your performance, and I heard mine. Sure, yours was a bit better, but we were very nearly equal. Bob said I did great, and I think you did great too. The judges preferred yours, and that's just how it goes. But you preened and bragged about that one point, and then two weeks later you started putting feelers out with your friends to ask my friends about me."

Like a forest creature in the presence of a predator, Rose didn't move. "You're angry that I beat you in a music competition?"

"I was fine that you beat me. Disappointed in myself, but whatever. That's what happens in a competition." He folded his arms. "What made me angry was how you tried to make people laugh at me. A year earlier, Mia had harassed my sister to the point of suicide. My radar for mean girls was sounding all the alarms." His shoulders dropped. "A girl bully understands only one thing, so I took my shot that way. I made my friends laugh at you instead. It worked. You left me alone."

Rose shrank into her skin. "I did do that, didn't I?" She sat against his rock, back to back with him. "I'm sorry. I was trying to get your attention."

"A credit to your skills. You got it."

She sounded plaintive. "We never saw each other except through the music school. The competition was practically the only connection we had."

"Walk me through what you expected to happen. Was I

supposed to challenge you to a piano duel to defend my honor, at which point we'd fall into one another's arms and then ride off into the sunset?"

Behind him, Rose remained silent.

Declan huffed. "Don't get mad. You asked, and I answered. My type is someone who doesn't stomp all over someone for social credit."

Rose spoke softly. "I'm not mad at you, but am I still like that? Couldn't I have changed in the last eight years?"

Declan tightened his hands. "Have you?"

"Having Mia do it to me showed what it's like from the other side. She was my friend, kind of. That's how she got close to Travis. They spent a lot of time together with me before they started spending time together without me."

Declan brushed the hair from his forehead. "That's a different kind of betrayal. As you said, you and I had no real contact before I shot you down."

Flirting. Covert glances. Third-party messages. And then mockery.

Rose sighed. "Friendship was always a commodity for Mia. The first thing she asked from me was access to a friend of mine, and every time she got close to me afterward, it's because she wanted something. The final thing she got from me was Travis."

Rose offered him the bag of cookies again, and he shook his head. She went on, "Back then I didn't have many friends, and the ones I did were...well, conditional. I moved to Hartwell when I was fourteen, and everyone already knew everyone else."

Declan said, "You knew the other music kids."

"They didn't warm up to me until I started saxophone and joined the orchestra. Before our piano competition, my friends knew I liked you, and they warned me not to play my best because guys hate it when a girl outscores them."

The hair stood on Declan's neck.

"I didn't listen. There was no way I would place higher than you because you were the best pianist I'd ever heard, except somehow I did. They were all over how I'd messed up any chance you'd look twice at me. I was supposed to throw it so you'd comfort me."

Declan huffed. "Guys aren't like that."

"Any girl smart enough to do better than a guy is also smart enough to look baffled and say she can't." Rose clasped her hands and stared at her knees. "That's what they said, and when I made it to finals and you didn't, they laughed that I was an idiot. They wouldn't let it go. I retargeted them to you."

Declan folded his arms. "Do you still think you're better than me? Not a better player. I mean a better person."

Rose huffed. "I never thought I was better than you. I played my heart out *because* I thought you were better. If anything, you've widened the gap."

She extended the bag of cookies again, and finally he accepted one. "Well, I think we're about equal now, and life isn't a competition."

She shook her head. "Back then it was, and I didn't know how to handle the judgment afterward."

Declan got down off the rock. "I'm tired of judges."

She reached for his hand. "I'm not judging anyone. It turns out not only am I a lousy judge, but I'm the least qualified to do it."

Rose scanned near the foundation of the house while Declan worked across the site by the footprint of what may have been an outbuilding. She'd rattled him. He needed space.

He'd have to return here someday. Even with two of them, they weren't going to cover all the ground he wanted to cover, and they'd discovered a thrilling haul so far.

Buttons. A thimble. Cutlery. A lock and hinges from a chest whose contents had disintegrated. A tool too badly decomposed to identify.

Even so, he couldn't focus. Why was Rose asking about his type? Was she feeling it too, that pull toward one another?

His metal detector indicated something awesome underground, so he used the pinpointer and started digging.

He wished he could pinpoint his own thoughts because if Rose was being honest, there wasn't anything standing in the way of taking things up a notch.

Maybe he'd just unearthed a treasure buried for eight years.

He reached the ash layer and kept digging until the dirt parted around a hard clump. He worked it with his fingers, eyes closed as he tried to sense through the ground. This was where being a pianist helped: he knew how to apply all sorts of pressure in different strengths, and he had good dexterity in his hands. Move it this way and that, shift, shift—and out it came.

The thing was flattish and rectangular. He pivoted it, tried scraping out the dirt, and then laughed. "Rose! I found a buckle!"

"No kidding!" She looked up. "Could you bring the pinpointer? I've got something here but no idea how far down it is."

He played with his new find while she determined she'd dug just to the side of where the object was. It was very close to the ash layer, and she went sideways to scrape the dirt away from her artifact.

"Oh. I thought it would be bigger." She came up with something tiny. "Any ideas?"

Declan rubbed his thumb over it. "A button, maybe?"

She ran the pinpointer through again. "Wait, there's more. Makes sense—more than one button." She scraped away more dirt. "Oh, gosh. Here." Out came another, and then a third.

Declan said, "Jewelry. I bet this is a brooch. Maybe a clasp."

"And this one's a ring." Rose sat back on her heels. "We found the remains of someone's jewelry box."

Half an hour's work turned up a handful of beads plus another ring and two more buckles. "Shoe buckles, maybe? Knee buckles? This is awesome." Declan wished he'd brought lights. Or maybe camping gear. He'd spend every weekend up here for the next month if his cousin let him. "I can't wait to get these cleaned up."

Rose came up from the hole with another metal bead. "What will you do with them?"

"My cousin and I agreed to split whatever I found. If there's anything valuable, he'll sell it. I'll post pictures on the online group, maybe keep a couple of things, give you some, maybe ask the local historical society if they have any input on who lived here and what became of them." Declan cleared out more of the hole. "You have no idea how amazing of a find this is. Usually a couple of buttons and a coin make it a successful day."

She sat back, dirt smudged on one cheek and her eyes bright. "You're saying this is a double amazing day."

"Triple amazing."

Eventually the pinpointer went silent, and the trove had yielded its last treasure. With their finds spread on a towel, Declan sat back to admire them all. "The rings are likely mourning rings. These two are probably brooches. The buckles could be for anything. I'm betting that's a cuff link, although we didn't find the second one."

Rose put her hand over his. "Whoever this was, they lost everything in the fire. Finding it today doesn't make up for what happened back then. Maybe they didn't come back to dig up their stuff because the owner was dead and they couldn't bear to do it."

"Or it was too dangerous." Declan shook his head. "We're assuming the structure burnt to the ground, but what if it stood for a while? Or what if there was a forest fire and the owners assumed everything was obliterated?"

Rose looked so sad. He put an arm around her, and she leaned into him.

His heart pounded. Instead of pulling away, she wrapped her arm around his waist.

Rose murmured, "I'm having a rough time with this pretend relationship."

Declan swallowed hard. "We're up on a mountain. Who are you even pretending for?"

She shivered. "I mean, I'm having a hard time keeping it pretend."

That was the push that sent him over the hurdles of his own self-restraint. Declan turned toward her and kissed her lips.

She straightened, eyes wide, breath suspended. With his heart slamming into his ribs, Declan managed, "I'm failing at it too."

She straightened up and returned his kiss, and this time she melted into his arms. He drowned in the sensation of her lips, the warmth, the feel of her against his chest. Like radio static resolving into the sound of a symphony, she emerged into his world with a crescendo he didn't want to silence. She filled his arms, filled his mind.

When he let her go, she gazed into his eyes, wondering and soft and delighted. "Action Item Eleven." She offered an embarrassed smile. "Be flexible about whatever happens."

"Affirmed," Declan breathed, and they kissed again.

CHAPTER TEN

Rose walked back into her house, dizzy, delighted, and determined.

And dirty. She had dirt everywhere—in her hair, under her fingernails, on her face—and anything that wasn't dirty was sweaty. She'd need a month under the hot water to shower it all away, and at the same time, she couldn't bear to let the dirt down the drain because it was a remnant of a day when everything came clean.

Declan. Bewildering. Thrilling.

Her lips tingled from his last kiss in her driveway. He'd promised to see her again tomorrow. He'd waited with the engine running until she got the door shut behind her.

Declan was for real. They weren't pretending anymore.

Sierra popped into the hallway. "Wow, you really did spend the whole day digging ditches! You're going to be sore all over tomorrow."

Rose removed her boots in the dooryard, then started

stripping off her clothes so she wouldn't track dirt through the apartment. "We uncovered so many things. You have no idea."

They'd discovered so much. She couldn't begin to process it all, so instead she stepped out of her dirt-covered clothing and headed for the shower. "I'll shake those out on the grass once I'm clothed again."

Sierra called after her, "Not a problem!"

Rose had been terrified asking Declan about his type, and then when she learned his rejection was in response to what she'd done—done to a guy who could nurture a grudge for ten years without breaking a sweat—that was the worst. Rose could have changed her hair color or worn heels if he preferred something cosmetic. Mia probably wondered why Rose hadn't done that already.

Then for Rose to find out she'd truly angered him, and then trying to escape that conversation, and *then* when she finally couldn't take it anymore and admitted her feelings....

That first kiss was ice on a burn. It was a cool spray of water on a broiling day in July. That kiss was the resolution to a fear she'd spent a lot of energy trying to forget.

All this because of his sister. Rose had wracked her brain trying to remember a Kimberly Hatcher from school or music recitals, but she couldn't come up with anyone. Kimberly, Kim, Kimmy... Rose had no memory of her, so it would be nice to meet her sometime. Maybe once she saw her, it all would come back.

Declan said his sister had left the Hartwell public high school because the administration hadn't taken any significant action about Mia's bullying. That meant it must have happened the year before Rose arrived. In Rose's first year, the district definitely had policies in place. Mia had actually gotten suspended after one incident, and Rose had barely escaped getting caught up in that dragnet herself.

The whole drive home, she and Declan had talked

nonstop. Declan apologized for misreading what Rose had said, but that was unnecessary. Given what happened to his sister, revulsion was natural. She'd stepped onto a landmine in his heart. Forgive him? Of course she'd forgive him. He'd done nothing wrong, nothing whatsoever.

With the dirt showered from her hair and body, Rose pulled on a hoodie and leggings, then went downstairs to hear the washing machine running and Sierra sweeping the tile floor of the dooryard. "I took care of it," Sierra sang out, even though it was hardly fair. Then again, Sierra's father was dying, and that wasn't fair either. "Tell me about the secrets the earth was keeping. Make me feel like I was there."

Sierra had already switched on the tea kettle. Rose was famished, so she started making dinner while she told the tale. Sierra looked devastated about the fire. "You didn't find a body, did you?" Her eyes were huge. "That would be horrible, not even knowing their names. How could you give them their peace?"

"We didn't find any bodies, but they must have left in a rush because Declan and I found what might have been a jewelry box."

Awestruck, Sierra drank her tea and listened to their finds. "All those beads," she breathed. "That's what life is made of—buckles and beads and brooches."

"Two rings, too. Declan called them mourning rings, but I don't know what those even are." Rose brought her spaghetti and pesto to the table. "He knew so many things it never occurred to me you'd need to know, like how to locate a three-hundred-year-old outhouse or how to tell whether a stream changed its course."

Sierra wrapped her hands around her mug. "Those really are the secrets the earth is keeping."

Rose said, "But there's something else, too."

After a day of digging and hiking, she wished she'd made twice as much spaghetti, and maybe ten meatballs too. Declan would have taken her out for dinner, except they were both filthy.

Rose steadied herself. "Declan and I became a couple today."

Sierra sat straighter. "You did? That's amazing! Isn't forgiveness wonderful!"

Rose started. "You knew about that?"

"I'm friends with his sister." Sierra beamed. "I'm so glad for you!"

Rose warmed inside. "I didn't intend things to go this way, but we were spending so much time together."

Sierra's eyes softened. "I only wish it hadn't started with an intent to deceive. That sets the tone for the whole relationship."

Rose shrugged. "If it hadn't started with an intent to deceive, it wouldn't have started at all. He was totally indifferent to me. But at least we never tried to deceive each other."

Drumming her fingers on the tabletop, Sierra didn't look mollified. "You're each aware of how the other one can lie. You encouraged it in one another."

Rose swallowed another bite of pasta. "I only did it because Mia was being obnoxious. We teamed up against her."

"You shouldn't care what Mia thinks about you. You're a whole person." Sierra sighed. "Mia is deeply broken. She's missing a piece, and she looked up to you because she admired you."

Rose snorted. "As if."

"You were her friend. Of course she admired you."

"When you admire someone, does it stand to reason that you steal her boyfriend?"

Sierra sipped her tea, then stared into the cup. "No one can 'steal' a man if he doesn't already want to split his attention. But I also believe someone who tries to 'steal' someone else's spouse or romantic partner—it's not that they want the boyfriend or the husband. They want your life." She met Rose's eyes. "They see you have good things, and they think if they can just land that guy, or that gal, they'll automatically get everything else."

Rose recoiled. "What did I have?"

"You have the whole package." Sierra smiled. "You had what looked like a good relationship. You had a band. You had a number of solid friendships. You had a job you're really good at, and you had the joy of your music. You had self-confidence."

Rose shook her head. "There you're wrong. I never had self-confidence."

Sierra rested her chin on her hands and looked right at Rose. "I'm sorry about that. But maybe now you'll see: Mia's opinion doesn't matter."

Rose nodded. "Declan's opinion matters."

Sierra's brows furrowed. "That's not at all what I'm saying. When it comes to being true to yourself—to the person you were created to be—no one else's opinion matters."

CHAPTER ELEVEN

What a dizzying array of finds today. A belt buckle, a jewelry box, and Rose's heart.

Anyone Declan had ever told about metal detecting thought it was about sweeping an expensive piece of equipment over the ground until you dug up a box of buried treasure. Likewise, they thought playing piano was about donning a tuxedo and striking all the notes on the page until the notes ran out and the audience applauded.

Outsiders never considered the "before" parts: researching likely places to scan, hunting down who owned the property and getting permission to go on their land, and determining how the land had changed. They never considered the "after" parts: identifying and cataloging the finds, cleaning them, and then dispensing them to their proper places.

As in music, there was plenty of excitement in the hidden work. For years, Declan had catalogued all his finds in a notebook, along with location, depth, site maps, and where he sent the pieces. The last page of his notebook currently said, "Wedding ring, soccer field B," along with a sketch of the park and Xs where his detector had pinged off something that seemed interesting but which the Department of Public Works wouldn't have allowed him to dig up. Unless someday they did—in which case, Declan knew exactly where to go.

On a fresh page, he included everything about today's venture with Rose—everything except the heart-racing parts. Everything except their mutual apologies and then her declaration of her feelings and then the most exciting kiss of Declan's life.

Now he sat at the kitchen table, having cleaned the corrosion off their shared past, ready to clean the corrosion off their shared discoveries.

This part took judgment and care because the techniques for cleaning copper were not the same as the techniques for cleaning steel, and everything was fragile after three hundred years underground. Unlike his feelings, which had emerged from underground with a volcanic ferocity.

While Declan cataloged and cleaned and diagrammed, he watched his phone from the corner of his eye in case Rose texted him. His shoulders and back were sore, but he was too excited to do anything other than work until two o'clock in the morning piecing together the past.

After a year of apartment-sharing, Sean knew Declan's post-metal-detection process, so he walked in and out of the kitchen doing his own stuff. Still, at one point he stood over the table. "Quite a haul."

"I'll need to go back. There was a fire, so they left everything." A lightning strike, a raid, an accident—who knew? Declan couldn't make that determination, but he was able to show Sean the clasp and hinges that must have been a lockbox, and he talked excitedly about the buckles, and then he showed him the contents of the jewelry box.

Sean snickered. "So, you're rich?"

"Hardly. Half of this goes to the property owner, and I'll split the rest with Rose because she helped."

Sean said, "Awesome hobby. You get basically nothing for all that work."

Declan said, "I'm a musician. Maybe I did it for the exposure?"

His heart and Rose's had gotten exposed. That alone made it worthwhile.

"Yes, and exposure leads to sunburn or hypothermia." Sean leaned over the table. "That's a buckle too? How many belts did they have?"

"Those colonials buckled everything. Shoes and knee breeches and on and on. I think this is a brooch, and these two are rings, possibly mourning rings."

"And a million beads."

Declan said, "There's always beads. Every human society that ever existed has had beads and beer."

Sean opened his hands. "There you have it. Add in some music and we're all set forever."

Declan beamed. "Finding a tin whistle or another brass instrument? That would be mind-blowing."

He closed his eyes and longed to bring Rose back to the mountain, but at the same time he didn't. Encountering that ash layer, he'd thought about the destruction of a family. A couple had hitched their stars to one another and climbed a mountain to carve a life out of the pine trees, and then disaster. Maybe their own disaster, or maybe something over which they'd never had any control. Maybe it was a careless stacking of logs in the hearth, or maybe it was something about the area they'd chosen to lay their foundation. Maybe their home had always been doomed because of something neither of them realized.

At least he and Rose had only good things left to realize. That was a relief.

His phone rang, and he jumped for it, but it was just Kimi. "Hey," he said as Sean left the kitchen. "What's up?"

"How did it go today? What did you find?"

This was another of the "after" parts, when Declan had

to tell everyone about all the bits he'd dug up. Even Dad's eyes glazed over, but Kimi loved to hear it. Sometimes Declan would send photos and she'd be on her end of the phone Googling while he was on his end entering other search terms, and together they'd identify something or someone.

The "someone" interested Kimi most. Kimi wanted to touch the same cup touched over and over again by a real person three hundred years ago. She'd hold a spoon and speculate about a flawed individual doing her best to thrive during a difficult time. Most of all, Kimi loved buttons. "Buttons hold things together."

They chatted over the speakerphone while he cleaned the pieces. "I can't wait for you to see. Half of them are going away, and I'll divide what's left with Rose."

"About Rose—?" Kimi sounded unduly cautious. "Rosalind Ward?"

"Yeah." Asking if Kimi knew her would be a ridiculous question. Everyone in Hartwell knew everyone else. "How'd you meet her?"

"Garden club. She'd just moved to Hartwell and didn't know anyone." Kimi sounded tentative. "I saw the picture in the paper, and she looks the same. Is she—? I mean, is she nicer than she was in high school?"

Declan didn't realize Kimi even knew about the piano competition, but that was the Hartwell rumor mill for you. He worked over the edge of a button with a toothbrush one more time before dropping it in the cleaning solution. "There were definitely issues back then. I'd written it off as irreconcilable, but we talked it all out today. She hates what she did back then, and she apologized for it."

"Oh, that's good. Maybe I should talk to her too." Kimi sounded relieved, but then the caution returned. "And you think it's legit?"

Rose's kisses certainly felt legit. Her apology had sounded sincere. Her devastation when he'd confronted her with what she'd done to him, and then her explanation about her friends—it was the full package. "Yeah. After

Mia hooked up with Travis, that was a massive wake-up call."

Kimi sighed. "It's a shame that's what it took."

Declan said, "But if Travis hadn't been an idiot, then I couldn't be with her."

"If Travis hadn't dumped her for Mia, you wouldn't need to be with her in the first place. Or are you two now a thing?" Her voice ticked up. "Really?"

"As of about five hours ago. That was part of clearing the air."

Silence, followed by, "Well, if you think she's changed, then that's what matters."

"She was scared to stand up to her friends. She admits that was immature."

Kimi said, "Just be careful. She still cares what her friends think, otherwise she wouldn't be doing this."

Declan said, "*I'm* doing this for you."

Kimi laughed. "You're dating Rose for me? My hero!" and then Declan laughed too.

He added, "I should bring her by sometime. Maybe for Mom's birthday. That way you two can talk."

"That's probably for the best. There will be a lot of people." Kimi sounded cautious again. "If you think she'd want to."

"Of course she'd want to." It was odd for Kimi to be so cagey, but she was protective. Declan picked up one of the rings. "I found two rings in the haul. Do you want one?"

Kimi said, "That's nice, but shouldn't you give them to your sweetie?"

"Two rings. Two people."

"Give Rose first pick. Although in the paper it looked like she already proposed."

"That was a photo op. She did it for laughs." Declan picked up the other ring. "They're tiny. Neither of you may fit them."

"People were smaller back then, right? Maybe you should sell the ring and give me another button." A pause. "Promise me you're sure Rose is really changed. You saw what she's capable of."

Kimi must have taken it to heart when Rose ragged on him. Declan dropped the rings into the cleaning solution. "It was high school, and you know how awful everyone was back then."

Kimi's voice was soft. "Yeah. I remember."

Declan first learned about the bullying after a Castleton Music School recital.

He'd spent the whole evening aglow with fury because his father and stepmother hadn't bothered to come. He'd been working for weeks on "Rhapsody in Blue". Every day he'd rushed home to study the music, or play the music, or listen to iconic performances of the music. He'd knock out his homework as quickly as possible so he could practice. That one piece had dominated his days and nights and all the in-betweens, to the point where Declan himself wondered if there was anything else he could think about.

The night of the recital finally came. They'd made plans to celebrate as a family afterward, but his family hadn't come.

Declan had worked the door taking tickets, and he'd hung out at the back long after the younger kids started their performances. They hadn't shown. Only when he couldn't wait any longer had he joined the rest of the orchestra in the prep room.

Mia Pratt sidled up to him and put her hand on his arm. "Performance jitters? You look so upset."

Mia had been flitting around him for a while, but with every day engulfed by "Rhapsody in Blue", Declan hadn't paid her any attention. He said, "No," and he went to get his music from his backpack.

She stuck with him. "Then what is it?"

Declan glanced at the clock. The violin trio onstage had

just finished their second movement, giving him about four minutes before he needed to go on with the orchestra.

Susan Castleton approached. "Mia, honey, we need you over at percussion," and Mia huffed but went to her section. Susan turned to Declan, her face softener. "I'm sorry your father isn't here tonight. Are you okay to go on?"

"Like I have a choice." Declan struggled to relax his shoulders enough that he'd be able to play.

Maybe his Dad and Mari and Kimiko had used a different entrance and he just hadn't seen them? Maybe they'd gotten into a car crash on the way over?

Susan said, "Take a deep breath and do your best."

"I hate this," Declan muttered.

She replied, "I hate it too. Sometimes the world caves in, and you still have to perform."

She sounded ominous. His hair stood on end.

Applause came from the auditorium. It was time.

Only when Declan took the stage in front of a full house did he wonder, with so many families here, how would Susan have realized Declan's hadn't come?

"Rhapsody in Blue" is an eighteen-minute piece, with the piano doing the heavy lifting. Declan had worked for four months on all the different segments, and the whole orchestra had practiced together for the past three weeks. He had to focus past the anger, past the anxiety. Pour the feeling into the music, but only the right feelings.

Afterward, he stood for his applause, hoping his family had arrived after he'd started. Bob Castleton (as the conductor) shook his hand, and Declan had the presence of mind to bow first to the orchestra, then to the audience. He couldn't pick out individual faces no matter how hard he tried.

Mom wouldn't have come. She hadn't turned up for anything she'd promised for at least five years, but Dad? Dad always came.

Declan's family wasn't at the reception either.

Unfortunately, Mia was. "You're amazing! I've never

heard anyone play that well!"

Before Declan could answer, Bob Castleton came near. "Mia, I need to talk to Declan."

"About his performance? Wasn't he great?"

"Yes," Bob said, and he waited until Mia withdrew. Still, she was watching. In a lower voice, Bob said, "I heard from your father, and I'll be driving you back."

Declan started. "What? He called? When?"

Bob pitched his voice low enough that no one could overhear. "Do you want to stay for the party, or would you like to go now?"

Declan huffed. "They'd better have a good excuse."

Bob's face was drawn. "They do."

Declan went cold. "What happened?"

Behind Bob, Sierra nipped around the buffet table and loaded a paper plate with cookies.

Bob said, "I'll explain in the car. Stay as long as you like, and then when you're ready—"

Declan said, "Take me now."

Sierra looked right at him with those piercing Castleton eyes.

When Bob signaled to Susan across the hall, Declan fought nausea. Had there really been a car accident? Was his father dead?

Sierra trailed them out the door to the car. Bob said, "Stay here."

Sierra didn't break stride. "I'm doing what Mom said."

Although puzzled, Bob didn't object. He took an immediate left out of the parking lot. Declan's home would have been to the right.

Once they were up to speed, Bob said, "Your father called right before the recital. Your sister is in the hospital for suicidal ideation or an actual suicide attempt. He wasn't clear, and I didn't want to interrogate him."

Declan sat up in the back seat. "Why? What happened?"

"I don't know, but it sounds like Kimiko is in good hands. Only, he and your stepmother are staying with her until the hospital can find a placement. Sometimes you get lucky and there's a bed available right away, but other times you have to wait a few days."

Declan said, "But is she okay?"

Bob sounded tense. "He didn't say if she needs medical care before they can transfer her to a behavioral health unit. Your father was distraught, and the only thing I could offer was to bring you after the recital. He asked me to record your performance though, so he could see it later."

Declan battled tears as he stared out the window. His sister had wanted to die or had tried to die, and Dad still hadn't forgotten about the performance.

Beside him in the back, Sierra wrapped her arms around herself. "This is awful. I'm so sorry, Declan."

Declan wouldn't look at her. "Your mother didn't tell you to come with us."

Bob's head swiveled toward his daughter.

Sierra answered, "Of course she did. Mom says that whenever you see someone's in trouble, you help."

Bob and Sierra walked Declan into the ER. A couple of words to the reception staff, and then Dad was out in the lobby, drawn, breathing hard, hugging Declan. "She's going to be all right," Dad kept saying. "I'm so sorry I couldn't be there," while Declan kept saying, "Is Kimiko okay? Can I see her?"

Finally Dad detangled one arm from Declan and shook Bob's hand. "Thank you so much for helping."

"Not a problem. If you want, I'll wait out here. If you're going to stay overnight, I can bring him home with me in a few hours. We've got plenty of room."

Dad said it was a wonderful offer, but no. Declan didn't want to leave anyhow. He wanted to see Kimiko. He needed to find out what had happened.

Before they left, Sierra handed Declan all her cookies wrapped in a napkin. "Give those to Kimiko. They probably didn't feed her anything decent."

In back, Mari was sitting at Kimiko's bedside talking to a doctor or a social worker or something. Kimiko had been crying, and Declan hugged her hard. She was stunned when he gave her Sierra's cookies. She'd never even spoken to Sierra.

One sentence at a time, Kimiko choked out that she was being bullied. At school. Online. Nasty messages from unknown accounts. Notes shoved into her locker. Girls inviting her to things and then excluding her. Girls who side-eyed her lunch and called it "meow chow mein". Screenshots from Kimiko's social media were being mocked on other girls' accounts—except Kimiko's social media was locked down. One of her bullies must be in deep cover as a friend.

Declan promised, "I'll end whoever's doing this."

There was no one to hit, though, just a nebulous cloud of social terrorists. But some names kept coming up. Mia Pratt, for one.

Kimiko went into a behavioral health unit for a week, and from there into a day program. She came home with medications, a therapist, and a lot of new protections at school. It wasn't enough. Three girls got suspended, but not expelled, and the rest didn't even get suspended. Mari homeschooled Kimiko the rest of the year, then shelled out for a private school.

Kimiko found a new friend: Sierra Castleton, who phoned Kimiko every day in the hospital, and then started visiting afterward. Sierra encouraged Kimiko to take music lessons, but when she found out Mia was enrolled at the music school, Kimiko refused. Even with Bob's assurance that he'd be vigilant, Kimiko wanted permanent distance from all of them.

To Declan's disgust, Mia Pratt dared to flirt with him. He shot her down, and for good measure he told his friends he'd rather die in a fire. Two years later, she tried again as if that was enough time for him to forget her knife in his sister's back. Again he made sure his refusal went through channels. Mia herself had taught him how to turn the crank on a rumor mill for maximum devastation.

After that, she left him alone. It had never seemed like enough revenge.

Declan's sister, however, had gotten the best revenge: she graduated college having rebranded herself. She emerged as Kimi, with a degree in human development/family studies. She worked as a one-to-one aide at the public school while finishing up a master's degree, with an aim to get certified as an occupational therapist. She also assisted part time with a social skills group for children.

She told Declan, "I wouldn't have discovered this if I hadn't started therapy myself."

To which Declan had replied, "That doesn't make it right."

Smiling, Kimi had taken his hand. "I can make it right for others."

Declan hadn't realized how he'd avoided "Rhapsody in Blue" until two years ago when he got tapped to play it for an orchestra in Bangor. During the first attempt at re-familiarizing himself with the music, he'd closed the lid of the piano and laid his head on his shaking arms. The anger. The horror. The hunger to uncover what was going on.

But then he did what Susan Castleton always said: you set yourself aside. You play. You play because that's what the performance demands.

CHAPTER TWELVE

It was still so hard for Rose to believe this was working out
—Declan, herself, Declan, Declan, Declan.

Rose entered the practice room to find Raf and Corwin
arguing in front of the white board—which wasn't unusual.
But they were excited—which was.

Raf brightened. "Is Sean walking in behind you? Please
say he's walking in behind you because we have awesome
news, and I don't want to wait."

Corwin snorted. "I plan to never shut up about it, so
who cares if we tell them twice? I got a call from a booking
agent, and you had better clear your calendar for a week
from Wednesday because we're the opening act for Vivid
Midnight."

Rose gasped. "How did you land that?"

Corwin said, "Friend of a friend, connections,
networking? The stars lining up? Maybe I sacrificed a goat
and forgot all about it? Whatever happened, I don't care."

Raf leaned against the wall. "What he means is, Vivid Midnight split from their record label to go indie, and they're showcasing a local act at every performance rather than being stuck with whatever band their label demanded they tour with. The owner of the venue tapped us."

Corwin said, "Whatever the reason, it's a chance to get in front of some major influencers and have our name in the paper."

Raf gestured to the song list on the whiteboard. "And I'm telling Corwin we can't cram fifty-five minutes of music into a thirty-minute set."

"It's not fifty-five minutes of music," Corwin muttered. "I do know how to add."

Sean walked in with his guitar case. "Oh, look, an argument! What a shock."

Raf said, "No, you haven't heard the shocker."

Rose texted Declan while they caught Sean up. "Corwin landed us a gig opening for Vivid Midnight!"

Declan replied right away. "When?"

"Wednesday after next." Opening for a national act like Vivid Midnight meant a large club or a small theater. She'd have to check the stockpile of merchandise to make sure they had enough shirts and CDs to sell. These gigs never paid a lot, but you were always looking for *the chance*. The chance to wow your fans. The chance to earn new ones. The chance to impress a producer or a record label.

Sean side-eyed Corwin. "And you haven't died of shock?"

Raf snorted. "No, Corwin dies of shock the day we open for Edgar Chantz. Speaking of which, don't you have a little altar set up to our favorite Castleton alumnus, with incense and a chalice containing your guitar picks?"

Corwin shoved his hands in his pockets. "I had to quit it with the incense because it kept setting off the smoke detectors—and no, I don't. Anyways, it's a six o'clock load-in. We're playing in Bangor, so we'll need to get there for a six o'clock load-in, and Rose, we need your truck."

Rose gave him a thumbs-up. "You always need my

truck."

"Your truck is the only reason we keep you around." He grinned. "That and your crazy keyboard skills. And your lyrical prowess. Oh, and your voice. Anyways, doors open at seven, and we're on at eight. We get thirty-five minutes."

Raf said, "And we do *not* cram in every single song we can."

Rose said, "Agreed. Let's work out a song list that fits neatly with the headliner, give a bit of breathing space between songs, and make sure the final song of the set has an incredible ending."

Sean said, "Thirded. I'm voting we start with 'Daybreak Nightfall', and we end with 'Somnambulation'."

Raf said, "Reverse them. That one ends strong, but it's not strong enough to get them out of their seats to buy merch."

Sean side-eyed Corwin. "And no Edgar Chantz covers."

Corwin pivoted, aghast.

Raf said, "Agreed."

Corwin rolled his eyes, then returned to the whiteboard.

Rose texted Declan, "We're on from 8 to 8:40."

Declan replied, "Let me know if you need a roadie."

Rose called across the room, "Delcan volunteers as a sacrifice."

"Accepted! We need coverage at the merchandise booth." At the whiteboard, Corwin returned to listing songs.

It was going to be a long practice session.

It was going to be a great opportunity.

It was a chance to perform for Declan, and that was better than everything else.

Rose stood at the head of the stage, staring at the mezzanine of the small theater. She'd performed in larger venues, but only during competitions. As part of Clear

Enigma? Never.

Declan drew alongside and followed her gaze. "You're going to crush it tonight. You're more than ready."

"If anything, we're over-rehearsed." She squeezed his hand. "Did you see Vivid Midnight backstage? They're amazing! I loved Scarlett MacNamara's chain mail jewelry. She's gorgeous."

Declan looked Rose up and down. "She's got competition."

Rose gave him the side-eye. She was wearing torn black jeans, black combat boots, a white tank top, and her cropped leather jacket—standard performance gear. She'd need to touch up her hair right before going on, but for the load in and sound check, she had it in a low ponytail to keep it off her neck. During performances, it raged loose.

Declan said, "If I have something for you, do you want it now, or after your set?"

She arched her eyebrows. "How about you keep it until after and only give it to me if we do really well?"

Declan shook his head. "If the audience is nasty to you, it won't improve matters if I'm nasty too."

"Save it in case the audience boos us off the stage, and then you can give it to me to cheer me up."

Declan snickered. "Well, it might cheer you up. Or it may make you think about death."

She laughed. "You've heard our music. Thinking about death isn't exactly a stretch."

Declan looked sly. "I'm counting on that."

Rose folded her arms and gazed back out at the auditorium, imagining it filled. "Now I'm intrigued."

Declan winked at her. "Memento mori."

Corwin tapped Rose on the shoulder. He was wearing jeans, work boots, and a t-shirt that proclaimed, *"Genius by birth. Slacker by choice."* "If the lovebirds would care to fly the roost, we have a merchandise table to set up."

Rose followed him to the backstage. "You've got nerve. You're the one who matchmade us."

"I had no idea how annoying you two would be." He

glanced at Declan. "No offense. You're selling t-shirts, so I can't complain too much."

Declan said, "Except you totally will."

Corwin flung open his hands. "Of course I will."

The merch table and wire racks went up easy because that was the same for every performance. Then, with the doors about to open, Rose found herself uneasy.

Declan said, "Stage fright?"

She shrugged. "Nerves are good. They keep you from getting complacent."

Corwin adjusted the position of the display t-shirts. "Nah, miss me with that. You need to quit caring how other people judge you."

Declan mouthed at her, "Corwin certainly did," and Rose smothered a laugh.

Corwin added, "If you wouldn't ask some rando for advice, why would you care about his opinions?"

The opening act was set up onstage in front of the gear for the main act, meaning Corwin and Sean would be positioned right at the stage's edge, and Raf's drum set went off to the side rather than directly behind them. When the doors opened at seven, Rose was at the table with her hair and makeup done and a smile for all the potential new fans and a number of old fans, several of whom Corwin knew by name. They didn't sell much before the show, but that was expected. The majority of what they moved would be between sets.

At seven-thirty, Corwin called to their band, "Time! Will the musicians and the drummer please report to the stage!"

Raf rolled his eyes, but a few of the onlookers laughed.

Rose kissed Declan. "Wish me luck."

Declan held her shoulders at arm's length and gave her a steely look. "I'm not wishing you luck. I'm wishing you the fulfillment of all your hard work."

She smiled. "I like that."

Warm inside, she headed backstage. The headliners talked to them for a few minutes, and Corwin shamelessly thrust one of their albums at them to ask for autographs. In return, Scarlett MacNamara handed Corwin one of Clear Enigma's CDs and asked if they'd autograph it. Corwin's eyes lit up.

Scarlett said, "When we're ready, I'll walk on and introduce you." At eight o'clock, the house lights dimmed. They took the stage. And they played.

They opened strong with Somnambulation, a high-energy youth anthem with a set of interlocking rhymes that had Sean working hard for every line, and with a closing crescendo that involved all four instruments. Corwin took the stage to say hello to Bangor and thank Vivid Midnight, and then he started the second song, a slower, grittier piece with a driving bass line.

By now Clear Enigma had the audience on their feet, so Rose concentrated on her playing rather than the heat, the way her hair got in her eyes, the way Raf wasn't quite where she expected him to be. At the edge of the stage, Corwin and Sean were blowing it out of the water.

Joy. This was joy. This was music and the reason she'd spent so much time indoors with a keyboard when she could have been playing soccer or hanging out at the shopping plaza.

The fifth song was a power ballad, and between Rose's keyboard and Sean's guitar solo, they carried the entire piece. During the bridge, Sean sang just at the top of his vocal range, and when he held one power note for long, so long, the audience screamed.

The closer was "Daybreak Nightfall". All four of them were singing on this one, all four together on the chorus and then that sweet extended ending with each instrument getting its own highlight as the song itself rose to a fever pitch.

And then, with anticipation cranked as high as it could go, Raf signaled with the drums—they played the final chord—and done.

The audience was bedlam. Sean raised his hands, and Corwin pumped a fist into the air. Corwin called off all four of their names, then thanked the audience, working the crowd even with them still thundering applause.

The volume doubled as Scarlett MacNamara joined them on stage. "These guys are amazing!" she called into the mic. "Don't you agree?" and that was heaven.

Amazing performance. Amazing feeling. Amazing everything.

Declan had watched her. That was most amazing of all.

Clear Enigma didn't do any real love songs. But over the moon as she was, Rose would have dedicated one to him.

Corwin, Sean, and Raf loaded their gear off the stage while Rose rushed to the merch table for the intermission. There was a line, so she slipped through to collect orders off the racks while Declan totaled them up and ran the credit cards. With only fifteen minutes between sets, the lobby thronged with people.

"Awesome performance!" one guy shouted over the din, taking both Clear Enigma's CDs. "Babe, you got someone to go home with tonight?"

Rose always said, "Nah, I'm good." These guys knew they couldn't rate the Scarlett MacNamaras of the world, but they might have a chance with the Rosalind Wards. As far back from the table as she could stand, she sold the guy his merchandise and signed his download cards, and she dismissed him without another notch in his bedpost.

The line moved quickly, and then Corwin was at her side. "Quit hassling my keyboardist," he snapped at one guy. "She's not for sale."

Declan reached around Rose to grab a bumper sticker. "Do they always do that?"

She huffed. "You'll notice I don't get too close to the table. I don't want to have to amputate someone's hand."

"No kidding. Maybe the fans are nicer in jazz piano."

Rose said, "Maybe it's because you're not female."

The house lights flickered, so they hurried the line through as best they could before Vivid Midnight started. Most of the crowd returned to their seats. With any luck, they'd come back after the show and buy more.

Declan processed a sale while a fan traded verbal jabs with Corwin. Waiting for the credit card to run, Declan said, "Can I give you your gift now?"

Rose grinned at him. "After-performance flowers?"

He handed back the guy's credit card, then reached into his pocket and pulled out a ring.

She gasped. "One of the rings we dug up?"

Declan winked. "It is if it fits. Otherwise, it's a charm for a necklace."

Rose had long skinny fingers. Even so, she could only fit the ring on her pinky. "It's got a death's head! I love it!"

The silvery ring was embossed with a cut-out skull between two leaves. Declan said, "It's a memorial ring. They gave these out at funerals."

Corwin turned. "What, really? That is beyond cool."

Rose showed him the ring, then flashed it at the remaining customers. Then, laughing, she kissed Declan.

Corwin snapped a picture, rolling his eyes. "That's not an engagement ring. It's just something you found in the ground."

Rose said, "Put it together, Corwin. Gold and diamonds came from underground. And here we are, an underground music group."

Corwin groaned. The lights flickered again, and the remaining fans scattered back to their seats.

Declan said, "'Til death do us part?"

Rose gave him a hug. "Maybe someday. Right now, it's about living and remembering."

CHAPTER THIRTEEN

Romance shouldn't impact one's ability to do math, but Declan had lost his ability to add. He was going to finish his Gilbert Ridge playlist with five minutes to spare. And why? Because Rose was sitting at a table in his line of sight, and she couldn't take her eyes off him. Nor he his mind off her.

It was unprofessional. Had he omitted a piece? Had he played everything too fast? He could pull something else out of his repertoire, but this was supposed to be his finale with a strong finish.

Strong like the finish Rose had pulled together for Clear Enigma. That still blew him away. At that keyboard she'd been so driven, her angry heart a channel between this world and a universe of musical energy.

He expected that anger from Corwin, who was sitting beside her now. He heard it sometimes in Sean, who wasn't in evidence tonight. In Rose, though, the anger switched off the moment she switched off the keyboard.

He looked at her again, concerned about those five minutes. He knew what he'd like to do with Rose for five minutes, of course. Five minutes together usually ended with his hands in her hair and her lips on his throat, but that wasn't good for a performance—and now their relationship wasn't a performance any longer.

His piece ended. Decision time. He gestured at Rose to come to him. She recoiled, and he leaned toward the mic. "Who wants a duet? Rosalind Ward? Would you care to join me?"

Her expression switched right over to her performance persona. He'd never witnessed the exact moment when Rose became Rosalind, but in one striking moment, her sweet eyes transformed into steel, her walk to a swagger.

"We're trying something new," Declan added to the audience, letting his voice go lower so it sounded smooth through the speakers. "Rosalind, do you like the Beatles?"

She said, loudly enough for the mic to catch her, "Everyone loves the Beatles."

He slid over on the bench, and she joined him in front of the higher notes. The silver memorial ring glinted on the pinky finger of her left hand, alongside his right. He said, "Do you have a favorite?"

She set her fingers on the keys, took a deep breath, and initiated the opening lines of "Nowhere Man."

The opening was a capella, which gave Declan eight seconds to figure out which key she was in and how to improvise the guitar line on the lower notes.

Improv was exciting. Improv alone, that was. Improv in groups could lead to disaster. Fortunately, the Beatles tunes mostly repeated the same chords, so once he got into the rhythm as the bass part of the keyboard, he could concentrate on following Rose's lead.

Rose worked the vocals on the upper part of the keyboard, a glint of her performance anger sparking through. Under her fingers, the vocal part became frustration with a person who refused to chart a path through life, less cajoling and far more urgent than the original.

Declan had never heard the song that way. In Rose's hands—Rosalind's—the song shifted from observation into condemnation.

As she glanced at the clock, he felt her calculating the seconds. After a rough transition, she started the vocal line of "Yesterday."

Yeah, give him a challenge. Every Castleton music student had performed "Yesterday". It was easy to improvise around the chords; the challenge was knowing when Rose wanted him to improvise versus when she wanted to do it herself. They needed to coordinate, but side-by-side, they couldn't trade cues the way a string quartet could.

Rose realized this the same time he did, because abruptly she switched into the "Long and Winding Road".

This song sounded glorious on piano, and it was already in Declan's Gilbert Ridge rotation. She and he blended, their arrangements coming together and parting and coming together again, until he could feel the length and twist of the road. The call. The yearning for something left behind, and the simultaneous tug toward eternity.

Abruptly Declan realized he couldn't hear the audience.

Nothing. No sounds of changeover. No patrons getting ready to leave or an open-mic crowd fussing to enter. There should be a musical act behind him preparing to lead off the night. The manager should be hovering, waiting to thank Declan and welcome the newcomers.

Instead, silence overhung in the dining room. Stillness from the bar. The only sound swelled from their four hands working eighty-eight keys. Her leg was alongside his, and every time he felt the need to press the damper pedal or the sostenuto pedal, her thigh shifted next to his and she did it for him. The dynamics were incredible. The song hungered to continue forever.

The clock hand ticked to the hour. Rose changed up to a series of closing notes, and Declan finished with the ending chords.

The audience exploded in applause, the first sound they'd made in minutes.

Rose turned to him with low-lidded eyes. "That's my favorite," she murmured loudly enough that the mic could catch it.

Breathless, Declan leaned in and kissed her, and there came a second surge of applause.

Rose brought Declan to the table where she'd been sitting with Corwin and Sierra. Corwin's shirt of the day proclaimed, "Underestimate me. That will be fun."

Sierra clasped her hands. "That was amazing!"

Corwin nodded. "My parents had a point about all those insufferable improv classes."

Declan pointed to the guitar case at Corwin's side. "What are you playing tonight?"

"Buckle in. You saw the review of our Vivid Midnight performance?"

Declan huffed. "As if I could have *not* seen it multiple times." He and Rose had spent a half hour quoting snippets to each other on the phone. While the reviewer for the Bangor paper hadn't said Clear Enigma was better than the main act, in three short paragraphs the review had hit every other thing you'd want to hear—on-point playing, terrific lyrics, and an excited crowd.

Corwin said, "The reviewer nailed it."

Declan said, "Your performance nailed it."

"Yeah, but he even named all our musical influences. Linkin Park. Coldplay. He compared us to Edgar Chantz!"

Rose winked at Declan. "Meaning now if Edgar Chantz ever searches on his own name, there's a remote possibility he'll read about Corwin and think, 'Oh, those Castletons, at it again.'"

Corwin arched his eyebrows. "I could contact him at any time on behalf of the school, you know. He's an alum."

Declan nodded. "Your self-restraint is legendary. Did the review mention your shrine?"

Corwin smirked. "That reminds me, I need to stock up on LED tea-light candles."

Rose said, "It's annoying that the only song the reviewer called out was 'Somnambulation'—and it's from the album with Travis."

Corwin rolled his eyes at Declan. "Back to my story, which you forgot you asked about. The esteemed Mr. Young got in my face yesterday about playing *his* song for Vivid Midnight, which he has no writing credit for in the first place, and he griped about the photo of you putting a ring on Rose's hand."

That photo hadn't gotten online accidentally. Corwin had posted it himself. *"Would you propose with a ring you dug up out of the ground? Rose's man has got a backbone of solid brass."*

"I told Travis what I always tell him. He'll get money for the album he appears on, and he'll get it when I do the accounts." Corwin drummed his fingers on the table. "I'm convinced trying to control us is why he refuses to let us buy him out, but he's the one who left. He has no right to say what we do with the band."

At Declan's side, Rose stiffened. What was she thinking?

"He ticked me off pretty good, and I'm about to return the favor." Corwin got to his feet with the guitar case. "Three acts to start, and then I'm batting cleanup. If you brought asbestos armor, now would be the time to weld it to your body."

Sierra sighed. "I wish you wouldn't mix creativity and retaliation. Music should be created because you love playing it."

Corwin smirked. "Well, I'm going to love this."

The waitress brought Declan a glass of water, so he settled in to wait for the fourth act. A high school trio sang a Taylor Swift song a capella. A man played a flute medley of video game tunes. A pianist who looked like he should be studying for a spelling quiz played Debussy's "Claire de Lune," and he did a phenomenal job considering his age—and his nerves. Declan ought to talk to the kid before he left, just to encourage him to keep going.

Then Corwin was up onstage with his Mustang and his amp and a live mic. Dangerous combination.

Someone called from the audience, "'Somnambulation'!"

"Yeah, no." Corwin finger-picked over the strings of the offset guitar, creating little blips of musical energy that weren't a song and weren't quite punctuation. "I need my crew for that, and you'll notice it's just me." While adjusting his guitar, he glanced at the audience. Was Corwin locating Travis in the crowd, or was he counting on the musical community to get it back to him? "I came up with a savage tune yesterday, and five minutes from now, my lyricist is going to wrench this thing out of my hands to shred it. This may be its only performance."

A bunch of cameras shot up to get video. Clever.

Corwin opened with a hard-edged, rhythmic tune, then backed off on the volume to start the lyrics. He could sing deep when he wanted, but now he softened his voice and worked in his upper range. The effect was breathy, urgent.

"It starts with a fire,
And a ring with a death's head.
A broken heart and a liar,
Their admissions all unsaid."

Open-mouthed, Rose snatched at Declan's hand and gripped so hard it hurt.

Corwin had put their whole relationship into a blender, and in chunks, he spat it into the lyrics. "A wedding ring lost." "One family destroyed and another one started." It was surreal. Declan could decode everything. Travis would get most of the references.

Corwin launched into the chorus, a powerful, "They think he's her...second cousin or something."

Rose gasped, shock rather than outrage.

"Second cousin or something."

Declan leaned toward Rose, who said in his ear, "Mia's going to flip her lid."

Brilliantly, Corwin had done everything so slantwise that his song didn't *have* to mean Mia and Travis. He focused a lot on the fire, on the search for what was buried. The destroyed family could be the one Rose never got to start with Travis—or it could be that homestead on the mountain. The song could be about cheating—or it could be about a nascent romance about to go public.

Rose wrapped her fingers through Declan's. She spoke again in his ear, her breath brushing against his neck so his skin tingled. "He gave us our own theme song, and it starts with a fire. That makes us epic."

Declan squeezed her hand. "I prefer happy-ever-after. Epics never end well."

CHAPTER FOURTEEN

Rose hopped out of Declan's Jeep holding his stepmother's birthday gift. The driveway was stacked three-deep with cars, with so many cars parked up the side of the street that they'd turned it into a single-lane road for any other hapless driver. With no sidewalks, most cars had one set of tires right on the grass, Declan's too.

Rose exclaimed, "There weren't this many people at the Vivid Midnight concert."

"Not quite, but Dad went all out for Mari's fiftieth." Declan took Rose's hand. "Tents in the back yard, a catered buffet, the works. Just for today, we're even allowed to wear shoes in the house."

Rose glanced at her beige pumps. "Thanks. If I took these off, you'd never be able to find me in the crowd." She'd angsted over what to wear, but Sierra had eventually loaned her a cream and brown knee-length dress.

Guests filled the foyer and the living room. As Rose left

her gift on the dining room table, Declan called, "Dad!"

Rose found herself shaking the hand of a man almost as tall as Declan, but not quite as built. Mr. Hatcher said, "Great to meet you! Declan told me how you dug up the mountain with him! I'd love to talk more, but right now I'm on a mission to bring up more ice."

Declan said, "We're not going anywhere," and Rose added, "Nice to meet you!"

The house was compact, the old but pretty furniture arranged with an eye for open spaces. Across the room, the wall was thick with framed photos.

Declan put his arm around Rose's shoulder. "Let's get something to eat, and then we'll find Mari and my sister."

"In a minute. Is that wall Memory Lane?" Rose's family also had a "Wall of Photos," with portraits of everyone going back four generations, plus pictures of friends and special events. It was neat that Declan's family did the same. If he and she went the distance, would they have their own Wall of Photos?

She crossed the room and zeroed in on a picture of Declan's high school graduation, and then another photo of him in a tuxedo at a performance. At the center was a family photo, with Declan and his father and—

—her heart stopped.

Declan and his father, with his stepmother and Kimiko Yoshida.

From high school.

That Kimiko.

Declan had called his sister Kimmy, only Rose didn't know a Kimmy, hadn't gone to school with a Kimberly or a Kim, so she'd figured Kimmy had been in Hartwell before Rose's time, then transferred to a school in Juniper just like Declan.

Hearing faded out as her ears rang. Sparks crowded out her vision. Kimiko. *Kimi.*

I have to get out of here.

The place was too full of people, the walls too close, the conversation too noisy. No one had seen Rose yet. Just the father. If Mari and Kimiko were in the back yard, Rose could leave and regroup, figure out what to do, explain. She could explain everything.

But to do that, she'd need an explanation.

Declan took her hand. "Are you all right? You're white as a ghost."

Her lips had gone numb, and she couldn't focus. "I'm dizzy. I need to get outside."

Declan sounded urgent. "Do you want something to drink?"

"No. I need to get out." Rose stumbled, but she made it to the front door and then down the steps. Her eyes burned, and it was so hard to keep breathing.

Kimiko. Declan was doing all this to settle up with Mia for what she'd done to Kimiko, only Declan didn't have the full roster of targets.

Declan needed to get revenge on Rose too.

Rose stood on the lawn, breathing through her cupped hands, fighting to get the nausea under control.

She had to escape. Apologize. Figure out how to make him understand.

Declan's arm went around her shoulder. "You're sick?"

She wouldn't look up, and his touch made her hair stand on end. "Can you take me home?"

Behind her, a voice said, "Rosalind?"

It was the same voice, eight years later. Rose clenched her eyes.

Declan said, "Can you get Mari? Rose isn't feeling well."

"No, don't." Rose pulled back. "I need to leave."

Kimi came down the steps. Rose hadn't seen her since she'd left the school, but Kimi was gorgeous. With her glossy hair in a French braid, she had poise, her eyes bright and clear. "Rose, it's okay. You can come in."

Rose edged backward.

Kimi said, "I knew. I talked to Declan. I saw your photo in the paper."

She'd talked to Declan? Had she wanted the fallout to happen in public? Or was Declan's real revenge in waiting for Rose to fall in love?

Kimi approached, hands raised. "It's fine. Everything's fine now."

Confused, Declan looked between them. "What's going on?"

With her mouth dry, Rose couldn't find the words.

The door opened behind Kimi, and it was her mother. Her eyes fixed on Rose, and it was the same effect as a laser sight and a gun cocking. "You?"

Rose backed away.

Mari pointed right at Rose. "You can leave. You aren't welcome in my home, and if you'd try coming here, you've got no shame. "

"Mom!" Kimi spun. "It's fine! I don't hold anything against her."

"I hold quite a bit against her." Mari stalked down the steps and stopped right in front of Rose. "I have no idea why you think you can walk in my front door, but you can turn right around and walk away again."

Declan said, "Mari, I invited her!"

She glared at him. "Do you care so little about Kimi that you've forgotten everything?"

"He hasn't forgotten! Mom, please, I'll explain." Kimi tried to get between her mother and Rose, but her mother wouldn't budge, and Rose couldn't get her legs to move. "I knew she was coming. What's she going to do to me?"

"Maybe take photos and send them all over the world?" Mari stared right into Rose's eyes. "Maybe lurk on Kimi's social media and sell everyone out the way you did before?"

With a sharp intake of breath, Declan drew back from Rose.

He'd realized. He'd realized in silence, but it resounded like a shotgun blast in her soul.

Mari glared at Declan. "You may have forgotten, but I haven't. There were four girls involved in harassing your sister. Four of them: Mia Pratt, Jody Olmstead, Heather Fontana—and Rosalind Ward."

With penetrating eyes, Declan was staring right at Rose.

Kimi raised her hands. "Mom, please, it's over. Declan said she's different now."

Declan's disdain slashed through Rose like a chainsaw. Absolutely, it was over. He might have said as much to Kimi before he realized—but right now, he didn't believe it.

Mari folded her arms. "Even if you're completely different, I haven't forgiven you. You put my daughter in the hospital. You used and betrayed her, and you never apologized. Even if she forgives you, I don't. You are not invited. You can leave."

Hands clenched at her sides, Rose backed up. "I'm going."

Kimi looked anguished. "I'm sorry."

Rose shook her head, but it was Mari who said, "You're not the one who should be sorry."

Rose went to the sidewalk, but Declan followed. "I'll drive you home."

His voice was cold. Rose said, "I'll walk."

Declan snapped, "Don't be an idiot. It's four miles. Action Item Two or something—I provide transportation."

They weren't an item any longer. It was back to items on a list.

Huddled in Declan's passenger seat, Rose couldn't bear the silence.

"I didn't realize Kimiko was your sister. You said Kimi. I didn't connect it."

Declan didn't answer.

"I wouldn't have gone." She stared out the window. "I hadn't even thought about her for years."

"Why would you? You never considered her a human being in the first place."

Rose's vision blurred, but she stared hard so she wouldn't cry. "That wasn't why."

"I should have put it together. Mia played you dirty, so I neglected to connect the dots that you were Mia's friend first. You were two peas in the same rotten pod, and you were just fine with the social bullying games until the minute Mia betrayed you."

Rose wrapped her hand around the seat belt. "I was never okay with what she did."

"That's why you fed Mia the screenshots from Kimi's social media? Because you weren't okay with it?"

Rose swallowed hard. "Do you want the whole story?"

"Not particularly, no."

Declan wasn't shouting, wasn't driving like a maniac, wasn't.... Wasn't there. As with his performances, he was invested in the act of hating her, and anything else didn't register. Declan's sister meant everything to him. You can't get revenge on your sister's tormenter by dating her.

You can get revenge by making her fall in love with you and then dumping her.

Rose shivered. When Sierra had said, "Isn't forgiveness wonderful," she hadn't been talking about Declan's *quintessential* comment. She'd been talking about Rose's role in the bullying of Kimiko. Sierra had assumed Declan knew. She'd assumed Kimi had forgiven Rose. She'd assumed Rose knew forgiveness was even required.

They were nearly home. Rose said, "Mia was crushing on you. She saw you talking to Kimiko, and she wanted to destroy her competition."

Declan rolled his eyes. "Because I'd totally date my stepsister."

"Since I didn't know Kimiko was your sister until today, you can assume Mia didn't have a clue eight years ago. Suddenly Mia started inviting me to her lunch table. I didn't have friends. I was new and awkward, so I went with her."

They were too close to the townhomes. Rose wouldn't have time to finish. "Mia had scoped out that Kimiko and I talked to each other, so she that's why she made nice to me. She wanted something. I'd seen what happened when people didn't do what Mia wanted. She spread rumors and excluded them and worse."

Declan huffed. "See, that much I remember. And it was acceptable to you that she would do it to Kimiko."

"I was scared! None of the teachers believed Mia did these things. She was a kiss-up student with good grades, and she was adept at social slights that left you feeling snubbed but never quite able to identify how. Other kids saw it, but they did nothing. I was just a transfer student. I didn't fit in, not even with the other orchestra dorks. She could make my life more of a hell than it was, or she could smooth it out. When she asked to see Kimiko's social media... I let her."

"Let me fix that sentence for you. You threw my sister under the bus."

Declan pulled up in front of her building. Rose said, "I threw your sister under the bus. It was her or me, and I betrayed her."

Declan's knuckled whitened on the wheel. "You picked the wrong side. You should have let Mia chew you up, because as it turns out, Kimi is *quintessentially* a better human being than either of you."

Rose's hands clenched. "I didn't know what Mia would do with the posts."

Declan lowered his voice. "Sure, you had no idea. You thought maybe Mia was stealing screenshots to nominate Kimi as Hartwell's homecoming queen."

Rose's lip quivered. "But that's all I did. Your mother went to the superintendent with a lawyer, and the other three got disciplined. The principal interrogated me, but in the end, they decided I hadn't done anything actionable."

Declan flexed his hands on the wheel as if he wanted to break something, then pointedly unlocked the passenger side door. "Not enough evidence to suspend you? That's exoneration?"

Rose had maybe thirty seconds before he kicked her out.

"I'm sorry. I'm sorry I didn't realize it was Kimi. I'm sorry I let you believe I had nothing to do with the bullying. I never thought about that incident because I wanted to forget about it. I'm sorry I hurt her. I don't know what else to tell you."

"You've said everything you have to." Declan looked at her. "You don't even get the worst part of this. Kimi was suicidal because of you. You might have ended her life. And in exchange for that—you didn't even remember her."

Rose's eyes stung hard.

Declan hadn't put the car in park. "Item Twelve: finish the performance. If Mia eats her heart out because you're with her former crush, that's what we intended from the start. We don't need to win any awards. We just need to play the final song and finish our set. No applause, no encore."

Rose twisted the memorial ring off her finger to hand it back.

"Keep it. Seems fitting now to have you wearing a death's head." Declan pointed to the door. "I drove you home. If you don't mind, I have a family to get back to."

CHAPTER FIFTEEN

Rose could feel Sean's eyes boring into her at the Monday night practice, and she refused to look at him.

A gleeful Corwin was bouncing around. "I'm getting so very uninvited from that wedding. Travis is beside himself, but if he says anything, he's admitting in public to his nasty behavior. Then to add insult to injury, I paid him early. I have definitely upped my pettiness game."

Raf gave a mini drum-roll. "Remind me never to get on your bad side."

"Everyone gets on my bad side. The idiots live there." Corwin adjusted a knob on his bass. "Rose, I need you to run your magic wand over those lyrics. They don't spark like when you write them."

How could she? How could she finesse lyrics about a relationship she'd destroyed eight years before it started?

Sean spoke in a flat voice. "I don't know if we want that on an album."

Corwin played a dissonant chord. "Mia may have scrawled that sweet tidbit on Rose's invitation, but it's not copyrighted. They have no claim whatsoever to the music, and there's enough other stuff in the lyrics—"

Sean said, louder, "I'm not sure we want that on an album. The bad blood isn't a good look, and we still need to work with the Tasers sometimes. We shouldn't force fans to choose sides."

Corwin exclaimed, "Whoa! Courage of your convictions, dude!"

Raf sounded puzzled. "We're not making anyone choose sides."

Rose sighed. "It's going to look as if we are. Sean's right."

Videos of Corwin's performance had popped up on the local music forums, with accompanying arguments about the lyrics. Fans had identified the ring within the first hour, but Corwin had steadfastly refused to clarify anything else, saying, "My dad swears that unanswered questions keep people talking, so I'm not decoding."

Corwin narrowed his eyes at Sean. "Did Travis tell you to nix the song? Because your longtime friend can go twist in the wind."

Sean kept his eyes on his music. "Actually, it was Declan."

Corwin turned to Rose. "He liked it! He was laughing."

Rose cringed as Corwin's eyes went to her hand. She wasn't wearing the ring.

"Blast." Corwin sighed. "Well, we'll table the song until you work things out with him. But get on that, okay?"

Rose slunk home, startled that it was still daylight. Summer had crept up on them, and she wasn't ready. Summertime was busy season for both the diner and the band. Corwin and Raf were calling every last contact so they could play gigs on nights and weekends until the supply of tourists dried up. Corwin wanted to hit it big before his father died. Given how Corwin was hustling, he must not think he had a lot of time.

An unfamiliar car sat in the driveway, so Rose left her truck at the curb. She'd slink to her room without Sierra or her guest noticing. Rose hadn't been hungry for days, so she'd camp out in her room without dinner until whoever it was left the house.

Instead, Sierra intercepted her at the dooryard. "Good, you're home. Corwin texted me that practice was over."

Rose avoided meeting her eyes. "I'll leave you alone. It's fine."

"It's not fine." Sierra waved her toward the kitchen, and at the table was Kimi.

Rose flinched, but Sierra said, "I'll be back in a bit." Then she was the one who vanished to the upstairs, and Rose was the one with the guest.

Looking nervous, Kimi smiled. "Can we talk?"

Rose didn't enter the kitchen. "Is it okay if I apologize? Because I owe you an apology, but I don't want to make things worse if you don't want to hear one."

Kimi snickered. "Rose, can you just sit down and talk with me? And yes, I will accept an apology."

Kimi was sitting in the place Rose normally took, so Rose took the chair where Declan had sat to work out their Action Items. The kitchen felt strange from this perspective.

Rose gathered herself. "I'm really sorry for how I betrayed you back then. I did everything wrong. I broke your trust, and I did it for all the wrong reasons, and then I never looked at what my deception did to you. I wanted to forget it, so I convinced myself what I did wasn't actually as bad as it was."

Kimi didn't seem surprised. "Apology accepted. Now will you listen to me?"

Rose owed her that much.

"I didn't realize my mother would recognize you, but I guess your face is burned into her memory. I hadn't shown her the picture in the *Herald*, and I never brought you up to her because I wanted to handle it myself. When I talked to Declan, he sounded like he knew everything."

Rose said, "Don't take any of the blame. None of this is your fault."

"Well, the miscommunication was my fault. My mother... Wow." Kimi flinched. "High school was horrible, but I escaped. College was totally different, and because I went through individual therapy and group therapy and a whole lot of work, I found a career I love. I made peace with the cyberbullying and the social isolation. My mother on the other hand has the memory of the goddess Mnemosyne, combined with the vengeful streak of Hera."

In Greek mythology, Mnemosyne had become the mother of the muses. Rose shifted uncomfortably. "I don't blame her. I just wanted to forget it ever happened."

Kimi said, "On the contrary, I don't think you should forget what you did."

As a lyricist, Rose picked up the shift from passive voice into active. "Why not?"

"Because forgetting our past decisions means we don't grow beyond them." Kimi paused. "You and Declan went to that dig site on the mountain, but first you mapped out where everything was. Why? So you'd know where to look. If you'd tried to sweep the whole mountain, what are the odds you'd have found anything of value?"

Rose furrowed her brow. "I see why you and Sierra get along so well."

Kimi sat taller. "Yeah, well, we're both a bit inductive. The point is, knowing where we failed shows us the weak places we need to repair."

Rose glanced out the window. "You're talking like a therapist. This is real life."

"When something is getting in the way of your real life, that's when you talk to a therapist. But I'm not your therapist." Kimi stood. "My mother returned your gift because she doesn't want anything from you, and you left your jacket, so I'm returning that as well. I've told Declan I hold nothing against you. Whatever happens between you and him, it's not on my account. I forgave all four of you ages ago because I decided it was healthier to let go. As far as I'm concerned, there's nothing on the books. Not with you, not with Mia. Go live your life, and I'll live mine."

Rose looked up at her. "How'd you manage that? The forgiveness, I mean. None of us asked for it."

"Unilateral forgiveness is a thing. Mia was tough to forgive, but you were the hardest. She was nasty from the start, but you betrayed me." Kimi headed to the door.

Rose looked aside. "I'm sorry. I did want to be your friend."

Kimi pivoted back toward Rose. "I would have wanted that too. Declan said you've changed, but in five minutes you've proven you haven't—at least not in any way that would matter."

Rose recoiled. "What?"

Kimi opened her hands. "You're not comfortable with yourself. Even though I know and accept the worst thing you've ever done, you're unwilling to look me in the eye. You're still hiding who you are because you want everyone to like you." And then she was gone.

CHAPTER SIXTEEN

Declan slammed the door harder than he intended, but whatever.

Sean was playing a first-person shooter video game. "Dude. That's not how you bring down the house.

"We're half the first floor in a hundred-eighty-year-old farmhouse. It's seen worse." Declan opened the fridge to find nothing he wanted to eat, shut it, and then looked in the pantry. Nothing there either.

Sean broke into a string of angry words at his game, and then he was back to running through ruins and setting his gun sights on shadowy targets. "Corwin agreed to table the second cousin song, by the way."

"Good." Declan looked back in the fridge. Still nothing.

Sean said, "For what it's worth, Rose agreed."

Declan had no energy for these gyrations. "I don't care what she's doing. We got done with the third-party message shuttling in high school."

Sean raised a hand. "She didn't tell me to shuttle messages. She didn't say much of anything."

Declan looked again in the fridge. "She's really good at not saying anything when it benefits her."

Sean huffed. "Look, I'm not taking sides or anything—"

"No, you never take sides." Declan turned to him. "You have zero convictions and make zero effort to stand up for anything you believe in, and that's why people get hurt."

Sean paused the game. "Who did I hurt?"

"People get hurt because bystanders watch when they get kicked and then don't help them back up again." Declan gestured at the game on the screen. "How many bystanders are watching you shoot the enemy there?"

Sean raised his eyebrows. "It's a game?"

"Life isn't a game, and people get hurt, and cowards don't say a thing. I was standing right there when you agreed Travis was a jerk, but you wouldn't *not* go to his wedding even though he cheated on Rose and tried to break up the band. You think you're keeping the peace, but you're just transferring the fight to other people who can't defend themselves."

Sean unpaused the game and kept shooting. "And that sounds like an argument where the other party isn't even in the room."

Fine. Declan grabbed his car keys and his wallet, and now neither party would be in the room.

At 1A, Declan turned east and headed for the coast. He'd find dinner instead of waiting for something edible to spawn in the fridge, only not in Hartwell where his music teacher was dying and a romance had died too. He drove away from Rose, away from the place his sister had thought of ending it all, away from the music school, away from his apartment-mate who so studiously avoided passing judgments and therefore engaged in the most cowardly judgment of all.

The silence bored into him, so he turned on the radio. "Kind of Blue" accompanied him oceanward.

At least Corwin wasn't going to blast that second cousin song everywhere. Fans of Clear Enigma were employed full-time in decoding the verses as though they were the clues to a treasure map. Declan had been identified, as had the ring. Maybe now Corwin would tell the fans to chill out because the romance had been fake from the start.

It was a performance. That was all it had to be. They'd needed to convince Mia and Travis, and they'd done it. Declan and Rose convincing one another had been an unfortunate side effect.

Rose, good at the role of making people think she was on their side.

And Declan, good at the role of....

Of what?

He sped through the gap between towns, trees whipping by on both sides of the road. These were the places drivers watched the brushline during the fall because a spooked deer might leap into the roads and wreck their day...or their life. Rose was a spooked deer. Deer never forgot that they were prey, except during rutting season when they forgot everything else. Rose got one look at Declan's family portrait and tried to escape the house. When she'd gone white like she'd seen a ghost, he'd thought it was the crowd or the stuffiness, except the ghost she saw was her own past.

If she'd escaped, would she have disclosed? Or would she have broken it off with him and buried the reason?

The towns came and went as Declan headed for the ocean. At Route 188, he pulled off toward Brighthead, one of the coastal towns that picked up a stream of flatlanders during the tourist season but wasn't otherwise much to talk about. He hit a drive-through for a burger and fries and drove his meal to the pier. Parked in front of a statue, he stared at the water.

The waves shuffled in, one after the next. You never saw them going back out again because that happened underwater. Instead the visible caps made an endless advance toward the shore without any gain.

It defied reason that Rose had tried to reverse the victim and offender. It was more convenient to forget her prey than to stare into the mirror and admit, "I am one of the predators."

Declan's phone chimed with a text from Kimi. "I saw Rose. I told her I've forgiven her and that I have no objection if you want to keep seeing her. I returned her jacket."

As if keeping a forgotten article of clothing would have been the worst crime in this whole monstrosity. Declan replied, "Why did you do that?"

"Because I want nothing to do with this. It won't help me to hurt her now."

Declan replied, "She betrayed you without remorse, and she deserves to feel hurt. All along, I've been doing this for you."

Kimi replied, "You're not doing it for me because it doesn't benefit me. You're doing it for payback."

Declan replied, "Payback on the people who hurt you."

"I removed myself from the equation. Get payback if you want, but you're doing it for yourself."

He dropped the phone on the passenger seat while he finished his burger. A mile out on the water stood the Brighthead Lighthouse. Bob Castleton had relatives in Brighthead, so one summer he'd brought the students to the bay for the year-end party. There'd been a cookout and live music because every Castleton party had live music.

Carrying the carton of fries, Declan walked along the pier. A statue of a woman stared out at the bay, a statue Corwin called "The Monument of Lies" because according to his cousins every detail on the plaque was wrong. Beyond that was a scenic overlook that took in the whole bay at once. The beach below was all rock, although the lighthouse commission had smoothed it in one place to create a zero-depth entry point.

At the Castleton party, the students had walked to the lighthouse. You couldn't do that now because the tide was too high, but as Declan watched the waves, he remembered the causeway. As the waters receded, a raised road of rock and gravel emerged. For a couple of hours, you could walk to the lighthouse with water lapping on either side. You'd hang out on the island, then hurry back before the water swallowed the path.

That had been so much fun. Lots of shrieking among the younger kids, afraid they'd get swept out to sea whenever a larger than usual wave lapped the rocks.

Declan stood by the lookout eating fries, hoping the seagulls wouldn't notice and commence the shameless begging. The waves kept going, and he let the sound soothe him.

Kimi was wrong. Declan was doing this for her. Even if she didn't directly benefit from Mia eating crow—or from Rose having her fill of just deserts—then Kimi still benefitted from knowing her brother had her back. It didn't diminish Kimi's past pain if Rose soaked her pillow in tears, but Declan dumping Rose proved that Kimi mattered more than a quintessentially not-his-type woman with a glaring personality flaw.

Kimi didn't want to feel guilty, and that was fine. Declan would accept responsibility for it all, for Rose's sorrow and for his decision to dump her. If anything, back in high school, he should have shot her down harder. If he'd known who she was, he would have.

The tide was going out. The causeway was rising through the waves.

Just like Rose's treachery, it had been hidden, but eventually it was bound to break the surface. Time would hide it again, but it would be there—waiting.

Seagulls began to gather, hoping for fries, so Declan returned to the car.

Kimi had no right to accuse him of doing this for himself. He didn't play games. He'd suggested one of Corwin's gang to pose with Rose, and then Corwin had nominated Declan. Declan had wanted revenge on Mia because he was angry. He'd been angry for eight years ever since his family hadn't shown up for their son because they'd very nearly lost their daughter.

He slammed the car door and left the seagulls unfed, then scrolled through his playlists for "Rhapsody in Blue". Kimi's words kept coming back to him, but he could remind himself why he was doing this.

The solo clarinet sang out as Declan slackened in the seat, eyes closed. Oh, that amazing opening with its energy and promise, the orchestra gradually adding support, and then the main line emerging like a causeway from the sea.

Like the fulfillment of a long-ago promise, the piano joined with a dusky opening to usher in the fanfare as the work truly began.

This piece brought back all the anger and frustration and helplessness. The isolation of knowing his father wasn't there for a really important concert—and then the horror of realizing Kimi might not have been there for the rest of her own life.

Kimi. Blast it, none of this was right. There was no question that Declan needed to get revenge on her tormentors. They'd abused her because it gave them a sense of power. Kimi was younger, and she was Japanese, and she was the recipient of attention from a guy their queen wanted to claim for herself. Kimi couldn't get revenge on them. Declan was the only one who could.

In fact, Declan should have done it back then.

And then his eyes stung because there were tears, and he screwed up his face to stop them. Because he should have done it back then. *He should have been there for her.* He should have noticed Kimi's increasing withdrawal. He should have asked about her social life and the torment happening online and in school, and he shouldn't have locked himself in his bedroom watching "Rhapsody in Blue" performances and reading up on piano technique and practicing all afternoon in the living room. When she sat alongside him on the piano bench, he should have noticed her sadness instead of showing off for her.

He should have been there for her then, and he hadn't been.

He wanted revenge.

He bore part of the guilt, but there's no vengeance against yourself. So many people had stood alongside while Kimi drowned, and no one had done a blasted thing —himself included. He'd dominated the whole family with his pride at being the soloist, and every night he'd talked about it *ad nauseam* while Kimi let his words flow around her like the tide. Every night, Declan had kept flooding into the empty spaces she left by her withdrawal, and she'd gone under.

He let it go now, cried in the car because if Mia had hurt Kimi by her action, then Declan had hurt Kimi by his inaction. And if Rose had betrayed Kimi by using Kimi's private thoughts as currency, then Declan had betrayed Kimi by not valuing those private thoughts in the first place.

Kimi was right. Declan was doing it for himself. He needed to make it right, only he couldn't give Kimi back those weeks, and he couldn't give back the years afterward. If back then he'd paid attention for five minutes, he would have been able to. He'd have stepped in and told Mia to knock it off. He'd have encountered Rose as Kimi's friend rather than as his musical competition. He could have culled Rose away from her fake friends. When Rose asked a friend of a friend to ask his friend to ask Declan what he thought of her—it would have been different. Quintessentially different.

Declan let "Rhapsody in Blue" run to the end. He squirmed inside, but he lived it. Through eighteen minutes of what was arguably one of the pinnacle achievements of modern music, he lived over that one season when he wasn't there, and he should have been.

Then it ended, its motif fast and energetic, then slowing and drawing everything into a tremulous fanfare that closed once more into silence.

He dried his eyes with the fast food napkins, then walked to the trash can to throw away a bag full of wrappers and unused condiments. The seagulls eyed him, still unfed. At the water's edge, he found a path fully exposed between the waters, straight out to the lighthouse.

He texted Kimi, "I'm sorry. Can I call you in an hour?" But then he turned off his phone.

He drove home. It was dark by the time he arrived, but Sean was still in the living room, playing his Super Strat as though performing to a full house at Fenway Park.

Sean pulled off his headphones, and their eyes met.

Declan shoved his hands in his pockets. "You were right. I was having an argument with someone who wasn't there."

CHAPTER SEVENTEEN

Rose stepped out the door for work on Tuesday morning to find Travis leaning against her truck.

Rose advanced, keys in hand, rage in her eyes. Travis had never physically threatened her, and it was early enough that if she screamed, all her nosy neighbors would run to the windows to watch. She wasn't afraid. Not exactly. Not afraid of what he'd do as much as what he'd say.

If an ex had to stalk her driveway, why couldn't it have been Declan?

She went around to the driver's side without acknowledging Travis's presence.

"What are you doing?" Travis followed her to the door. "What's your game?"

"You mean the game of moving on even though you're getting married in a few weeks?"

Travis folded his arms. "Why do you pretend like I'm

stupid? You're grandstanding, and it's frankly embarrassing. People have been asking me if marrying Mia is upsetting to you."

People were asking *Travis* about her? What even gave them the right?

Rose got into the seat. "I can't see how my being upset would in any way be your business. Back away unless you want me to drive over your foot. I want nothing to do with you."

Travis backed up. "When you broke up with me, you said we could be friends, but this isn't friendship. We never talk, and now you're becoming unhinged."

For the first time, she looked at him directly. "You chose this. I abided by your choice."

His brow furrowed. "Thank you for talking to me. And you don't hate Mia?"

"In case you hadn't noticed, Mia hates me. And you can tell the entire concerned population of Hartwell that Corwin wrote his song without any input from me. He takes pride in being unhinged."

"Yeah, he said." Travis's expression softened. "Rose, I'm not here just because other people are concerned. I'm worried about you too. I miss the friendly Rose who used to talk to me at the end of the day, who used to jam with me and go to concerts with me."

Rage burned in the top of her throat. "Again, I can't see how that's my business. You cheated with my friend, lied for two months, and then dumped me."

Travis raised his hands. "I wasn't cheating."

"And now you're lying again. Since you're asking about my game, what's your game? Why are you here?"

Travis dialed up the charm. "I'm afraid I shattered you. You never let me clear up the misunderstandings when you dumped me. That haunts me all the time, and I want to make it right. I don't want you to walk all the way out of my life. A part of my heart stayed with you, and I can't let you make a mistake like being with Declan just to spite me."

She stared at him. "Have you listened to yourself?"

Travis stepped closer. "You don't have to stay away the way you have been. We meant so much to each other. We still can. I want you to talk with me sometime. We'll watch TV and have dinner, maybe play music again. That doesn't have to end."

Rose's hand clenched around her keys, clenched until it hurt because that pain was an honest pain. That pain was reality, whereas Travis standing here, testing the waters, was delusion.

Declan had dumped her because in eight years Rose couldn't possibly have changed, and here stood Travis, betting Rose was still the same easily-deceived girlfriend with a wound in her heart. "Are you going to ditch Mia? You'll call off the wedding so you and I can cuddle on your couch to watch livestreamed concerts from California clubs?"

Travis's eyes narrowed. "Maybe you're what's been missing all along."

"Maybe you should have thought of that two years ago, when you believed what was missing was the excitement of juggling multiple girlfriends."

He glared at the sky. "I don't understand why you're being so hostile. Are you really one of those girls who never lets go of the past? My friends are frankly shocked that you're behaving this way. They didn't think you were like all the other girls. They thought you'd be mature and not slam the door just because you couldn't get everything you wanted."

It was a good thing Travis wasn't standing right in front of Rose's truck because she'd never have been sure afterward that she hadn't meant to run him down. Rose turned on the engine. "Raf told me that when a guy marries his affair partner, he's only creating a job opening. I don't intend to fill it. If you want to cheat on Mia, it won't be with me."

She slammed the door and put the truck in gear. She had to glance at Travis long enough to make sure she wasn't really going to drive over his foot, and then she drove to work battling tears.

Declan hated her. Travis was doing...whatever Travis was doing. Mia despised her. Kimi should hate her but didn't. Kimi's mother? Loathed her. Maybe Mari had started the smear campaign Travis mentioned, assuming Travis hadn't made the whole thing up. Sierra didn't hate Rose—but Sierra loved everyone with the passion of a star child who beheld each soul's true potential, so that didn't count. Sean never took sides. Corwin liked her, but Corwin also loved stirring up trouble. If Corwin encountered any rumors that Rose was unhinged, he'd encourage them.

Raf was okay with her, at least. Raf was normal enough.

Travis made it sound as if everyone in Hartwell thought a semi-sane Rose was bleeding out through a heart with multiple fractures. Travis wanted to pick up the pieces, and Declan wanted to kick them around in the gutter.

So what do you do? Susan Castleton would have said you continue the performance, no matter what. Get out in front of them and give them the music. Sudden death was the only valid reason not to perform.

How was Rose supposed to attend a wedding with Declan and hold his hand, knowing he'd rather hold a rattlesnake? How could they slow-dance the required three times, his heart against hers, and not have it gut her like a fish?

How could she pretend to love him when she did love him?

How could she pretend to love him when he'd be pretending the same, only he didn't?

And Travis? Why the proposition that since she couldn't be his primary, she could be his side piece? Why the shot at Declan? Travis had started by asking what Rose's game was, when all along he was the one playing. Travis loved this kind of game, where she didn't know the rules, didn't know the victory conditions, and didn't even have a playing piece.

At the diner, Rose struggled to focus on all the opening

tasks. Larry had logged onto the computer in the office, so Rose couldn't do inventory right now. Instead she resolved a schedule conflict for the afternoon employees, then went into the walk-in to check out a customer complaint about spoiled strawberries.

It was too bad she couldn't leave her brain in the fridge. Let it chill while she did her job. Maybe she should leave her heart in the freezer, too.

If the point of this mess was to get even with Mia, taking Travis back would do nicely. But that meant being with Travis, and...well, why? Why stay involved when every player hated every other player?

One of the waitresses poked her head in the walk-in. "Guess who's here?"

Rose closed her eyes. "Shoot me now."

The waitress snickered. "I'm not that kind."

Rose went to Mia and Allison's table. "Morning. What can I get you?"

"Coffee," Mia said. "But I want the strongest coffee you have."

Allison added, "Only if it's fresh. Is it fresh?"

"It's brewing right now." Rose clicked into autopilot. "Do you know what you want to order?"

Mia said, "You haven't even brought us a menu."

Rose went to get two menus, noticing the coffee had just finished dripping into the pot. Mia would expect her to move the pot to the other burner and start a second one just for her. Sure, let everyone else have slightly-weaker, somewhat-stale coffee.

Enough.

Rose filled two coffee cups with regular coffee and brought them and the menus to the table.

Allison muttered, "*That* was fast."

Mia stared right at Rose. "Why was Travis at your house this morning?"

The muscles tensed in Rose's shoulders. "I have no idea."

"You know what I'm talking about."

"I know he was there. Were you following him?" Rose's eyes widened. "Do you have a location tracker on his phone? Are you saying you don't trust your own fiancé?"

Rose was dangerously close to laughing—the kind of helpless laugh that emerges when the world's absurdity has rocketed beyond anything you were ever prepared to handle.

Mia raised her voice. "Don't put this on me. Why are you trying to seduce my boyfriend?"

Well, that had the attention of every single patron. "You should ask him why he parked at my curb in the small hours of the morning. He'll tell you he remembered last night that I never returned his Life of Agony concert t-shirt." Rose pulled her pad and pen from her pocket. "Are you ready to order?"

Mia said, "I'm ordering you away from Travis."

"Wouldn't it be more effective to order Travis away, since he came to me?" Rose looked her in the eye. "I asked, are you ready to order?"

The tension had traveled down Rose's shoulders to her hands, up her neck all the way to her eyes. If flames shot from her hair, it wouldn't have surprised her at all.

Mia was projecting her voice. "Do you really want to play it this way? Because I can take you down. I know everything about you."

By contrast, Rose lowered hers. "I know plenty about you too. They call this mutual assured destruction. Are you ready to order?"

Mia's hands tightened. "You're doing everything possible to get his eyes on you. You've always been an attention queen. Writing a song about him?"

"Corwin wrote that song. He thought it was hilarious that you believed Declan was my second cousin or something, especially since you don't even know who Declan's sister is." Rose put the pad and pen back in her pocket. "Since you're not ready to order, I'll be back in five minutes."

Mia said, "Who's his sister?"

Rose made sure she was looking right at Mia. "Kimiko Yoshida."

Horror flashed over Mia's eyes.

Rose added, "He has never forgiven you."

Mia frowned. "But he forgave you?"

"We're not a couple anymore. Read into that whatever you like." Rose folded her arms. "Don't worry. I won't bring my second cousin to your wedding. I just won't show."

Mia pointed at her. "You're wasting my money. You already RSVP'd for two people."

Rose shrugged. "You won't have turned in a final headcount yet, and I'm done. I'm done with your mockery, your nastiness, your superiority, and your head games. If you want to trash my reputation to the whole music community, go ahead. It's no worse than either of us deserves, and I should have done it myself long ago. Maybe if I had, Travis wouldn't have decided to cheat."

Mia's eyes flared, and Rose realized too late what she'd said versus how Mia had heard it. Not that Travis had cheated on Rose with Mia—because that wasn't something Mia cared about. No, Mia had heard that Travis was cheating *now*. Declan had just left the relationship, therefore Travis was cheating *now,* with Rose.

Allison said pointedly, "You know, this coffee isn't strong at all."

Mia grinned. "Really? The manager of a diner can't even make a decent cup of coffee?"

A year after she should have, Rose finally said, "They make coffee up the street, you know."

Mia raised her voice. "I want to talk to the owner. You've been arguing with me for five minutes, haven't taken our orders, didn't have menus for us, and gave us disgusting coffee."

Every customer was taking in the free show. Rose said, "With pleasure," and strode to the desk at the back.

Larry was glaring at Rose before she even reached him. "Why are you letting her shout? Give her whatever she wants, for crying out loud."

"What do you think I'm doing?" Rose pointed toward the table. "She wants you."

Larry heaved himself out of the desk chair. "Don't go away. You're not getting out of it this easily."

Rose was about to get fired.

Mia would smear Rose's name all over town. Maybe Mia was already the one smearing her. The music community in Hartwell knew them all, though. They'd laugh it off, and then when something else grabbed their attention, they'd laugh about that instead. Mia would spend every night of her marriage hunting for infractions on her husband's phone, and Rose would have a reputation as an unemployed, unhinged, social media bully.

At the table, Mia spewed out a long list of Rose's travesties while the spectating customers fought laughter. Larry sighed and offered lame apologies, offered to comp Mia's breakfast (of course he did) and then turned to Rose.

Rose said, "I'm not doing it. I'm not rewarding her anymore for being a bully. Enough is enough."

Larry bristled and drew breath to speak.

Behind Rose, one of the waitresses said, "Excuse me, sir? But table five's meal is about to come up, so you'll want to keep an eye out for that."

Startled, Larry said, "What?"

"Because if you fire her, I'm walking out right behind."

The second waitress appeared on Rose's other side. "Table one is going to need a refill on their coffee. Theirs came from the same pot, by the way, and they said it's fine."

The cook called from the kitchen, "Also, you're going to want to get these waffles before they burn."

The breath caught in Rose's throat.

Mia quivered. "I will tell everyone. I will trash this place online and make sure everyone knows."

Larry returned to the familiar role of de-escalating a customer. "That isn't necessary. Now, what was it you wanted?"

Rose said, "She wants to destroy me because her fiancé propositioned me in my driveway, but she'll settle for very strong coffee that's not espresso. Mention that in your review. 'One star. Drama-llama waitress. Lousy coffee.'"

Mia slammed her hand on the table. "You need to lose your job."

Rose smirked. "As I said to Travis, you do have a talent for creating a job opening."

Mia got to her feet, but Larry stepped in between them. He turned to Rose.

This was it. She was getting fired, but at least she'd stood up for herself first.

Larry murmured, "Please return to the kitchen." Then to the two waitresses, "Please check on your tables." And finally he turned to Mia and Allison. "Please leave my diner."

It took a moment for Rose to parse his words, and it took Mia that same moment. Mia's mouth opened, and Larry raised a hand. "You aren't coming here for the food. You're coming to create a scene. I'm done letting you use my staff for your self-gratification. Feel free to leave all the nasty reviews you want in as many places as possible. Thank you for your patronage."

Behind Mia, one of the customers gave Rose a thumbs-up.

They'd seen her. They'd seen everything, heard everything, and somehow they hadn't turned against her.

Mia grabbed her purse. "This isn't over."

It would never be over, no. But a few things were over as of this moment. One of them was Rose's silence.

In the kitchen, she leaned against the wall, and with shaking hands, she texted Corwin. "Send me a copy of that song. I'm going to polish up the lyrics."

CHAPTER EIGHTEEN

On Thursday night, the Gilbert Ridge Bistro had a decent crowd, and Declan felt every pair of eyes watching, every pair of ears listening. Rose said when he played, he wasn't there. Tonight, he was trying to be here.

Clear Enigma sat at a table together. Rose had texted that they'd be coming. In fact, she'd texted him a bunch of things, all business items that might as well have begun with, "To whom it may concern."

"I uninvited us from Mia's wedding, so you don't have to worry about that anymore."

"I told her we're not together right now, so likewise."

"CE will play at the open mic. Don't be surprised when you see us there."

He hadn't replied to any. Well, hadn't replied with a text, that is. He'd certainly replied by ranting in private. "We were doing this for a reason," he'd griped while fixing an air conditioning unit. "We had a plan, and just because you can't get exactly everything you want doesn't mean you get to flounce out of the whole thing."

Now they had nothing to show for this goat rodeo. No "eat your heart out on your wedding day, Mia Pratt-Young." No shielding of Rose from her former friend's judgmental eyeballs. No shot at Travis that his ex was living well. The worst possible outcome—the very worst, as far as Mia and Travis were concerned—was they had to adjust their final headcount. For a buffet. That was still weeks away.

And then that last text, as though the problem with Rose invading Declan's space was Declan's potential surprise, not that she had no idea how to bury a dead thing. She forgot the things she needed to remember and killed the things she needed to keep alive.

For all that, he missed her.

He missed her as he played "Yesterdays," and he missed her when he played the Rondo Alla Turca, and he missed her when someone requested a Beatles song.

Her three messages might mean she missed him too. Which was good because she deserved to suffer.

He was aching too. Maybe he also deserved it.

Declan had played every song tonight anticipating that she'd make a request to up the stakes. Maybe "Please Forgive Me," or if she was angry, "Cold as Ice." Instead there was quiet from the Clear Enigma table.

Rose was quintessentially not his type. The "quint" essence, the fifth element behind earth, air, fire, and water. It was the aether that flowed through the universe, breathing spirit into the world, bestowing meaning on it all.

If Rose was quintessentially his type, then their essences were the same. Back then, she'd been absorbed with saving herself, and he'd been absorbed with being himself. Kimi had become the lightning that ignited the aether and left it blazing like a torch in a parapet.

It didn't matter. Declan couldn't get past what Rose had done to Kimi. How could he? Except that Kimi herself had gotten past it.

His fingers moved over the keyboard by pure muscle-memory. Could Rose hear him emoting through the music? If he played a lively song, did she hear the underlying pain? When he played something thoughtful, did she hear his sadness?

Could she answer his question for him, then? Whether he wanted to move past her betrayal or whether he wanted to clench his fists on the judgment?

He kept telling himself that dropping convictions because they're inconveniencing you means they're not convictions. Then they're just wishes, and wishes never helped anyone. Just because he wasn't there then for Kimi didn't mean he was required to be here now for Rose.

Declan concluded his set, and the manager went to the mic. "Thank you so much! We're beginning our open mic night, but since Declan will be playing for that as well, we'll keep him up here for the moment."

Declan turned to the manager to ask what on earth that was about, when behind him he saw Clear Enigma.

Corwin seized the mic. "We'll take a minute to get set up, but you know us. We're worth waiting a whole minute." Laughter filled the dining room.

Rose offered Declan some sheet music. "This was Corwin's idea," she said low enough that the mic couldn't broadcast it. "He didn't tell me until two minutes ago when I asked how he'd seized the first slot. He did it by telling the manager you'd already be onstage, so bump everyone else."

Declan said, "And if I run?"

"Then Corwin looks like a jerk, and I play the piano."

Sean came up to Declan. "Do it."

Raf added, "Trust us. Do it."

Corwin's sister Lindsey joined them with an electric violin while Corwin was saying, "While I hate setting the bar so high for everyone who comes after us, I don't actually hate it enough not to. Please hold your applause until the end."

Lindsey said, just loud enough for the mic to catch it, "That'll help you maintain your humility," and the audience hooted.

Declan studied the untitled sheet music a moment, then recognized the song: it was Corwin's Mia-mocking "Second Cousin or Something," now with a piano line.

He handed it back. "I'm out."

Sean said, "I'm telling you to trust me."

Rose rubbed her hand. "I rewrote it."

She wasn't wearing the death's head ring.

Raf didn't have the full drum set, just one. Lindsey had plugged into an amp next to Corwin's.

Declan got closer to Rose. "You said we're out of the game. We're disinvited."

She shifted her weight. "I changed the whole song." Her eyes were shining, and her face was devastated.

The audience was settled in, and Corwin watched the standoff while hammering individual notes up and down the fingerboard. Lindsey adjusted her tuning, buying time. Meanwhile Rose looked breathless and small. He recalled her huddled in the front of his truck, trying to explain the inexplicable, struggling to soothe her conscience over the unconscionable. Trying to coax him to love the unloveable.

She'd come to him despite his refusal. She'd shown up, fully present. He couldn't know for sure that she'd changed, but he'd changed. He hadn't been there for Kimi, but whatever happened with Rose tonight, he should at least be here to witness it.

Declan plucked the music from her hands.

A baby grand wasn't Clear Enigma's typical sound, but listeners at an open mic night got what they got. For example, an electric violin. Declan spread out the pages on the music stand, and joy, Rose had streamlined it for sight-reading purposes.

Sean and Corwin set up on either side of the mic so they could share, and Rose had a mic of her own. Corwin laid down a few opening chords on the bass, and then Sean took over the melody. The revised song had a slower tempo. Declan and Raf joined, and Lindsey accented the main line.

Although Sean was Clear Enigma's lead singer, tonight it was Rose. She boosted herself onto the side of the piano to project her voice without Corwin's anger.

"It starts with a fire,
And a ring with a death's head.
He doesn't know I'm a liar,
Both a spy and a bad friend."

It was a good thing she'd streamlined the keyboard part because otherwise Declan would have stopped playing.

Rose sang in a breathy voice, sang about herself. *"A friendship destroyed, and a romance I've gutted."*

Declan wanted to stop her—stop Rose now before she shoved his sister back into the spotlight. How dare she profit off Kimi yet again? Somehow, though, Rose kept the focus off Kimi and where it needed to be—on a person who'd traded friendship for safety and then traded honesty for appearance.

Corwin's lyrical shots at Travis transformed into a tragedy. In her lyrics, Declan and Rose were back on that mountain, *"unearthing the past from a layer of ash, standing on gravesites, love devoured by unknown corrosion."*

Rose's voice filled the room. *"And it's all very fragile."*

Manipulating emotions was her job, and maybe she was trying to manipulate his. Maybe she was succeeding.

"Dig into the past, and sometimes you find death."

Clear Enigma broke into a bridge that hadn't been part of the original, and here Lindsey took over with the electric violin. She and Corwin played back to back, him laying down a complex counterpoint to her keening high notes. Lindsey's violin broadcast despair, and Corwin's bass growled out a frustration of its own.

That frustration echoed the one in Rose's voice. It was the same loathing Declan had felt toward himself on the Brighthead pier.

"I can't ask his forgiveness.

And you know I deserve this."

She'd poured her failure into the song. An awkward newcomer, a struggle to protect herself, a lousy decision made for the wrong reasons...and no way out once it was made.

"Now he acts like I'm a...second cousin or something. Second cousin or something."

The song closed. Legs dangling, Rose sat on the piano with her hands gripping the lid, shoulders slumped, head down.

Watching her, it took Declan a moment to hear the applause.

Rose had just trashed her own reputation. If she was worried about what people thought of her, she'd just handed over all the fodder they needed to despise her forever.

He gave his hand to help her down. She stepped into his arms, and they hugged.

She fit so well. She always had.

The rest of the band started clearing the stage, but Declan didn't want to move. Once he moved, the enchantment would shatter.

She stepped back, and he saw she was wearing the ring on a chain. He touched it.

Rose shivered. "Dig into the past, and sometimes you find death."

Declan said, "I'm beginning to think the best thing you can do with the past is to dig it up."

They walked the shoulder of the state route away from the Gilbert Ridge, one in front of the other, cars zipping past. They needed to talk, and Declan didn't know how to start the conversation, nor what even to say.

At the first side street, Rose turned away from the noise

of the main road, and they walked through a residential area. The road had been patched so much it was barely paved. The houses had lights in the windows, but there were no sidewalks. Now they could walk side by side on the untraveled street. The further they went, the fewer sounds Declan could hear.

Declan could say, "It was nice of Lindsey to play with you," or "Why did you tell Mia we weren't coming to her wedding?" He could say, "It was a jerk move for Corwin to use me to get the first slot, but I guess he wanted to make sure I heard the song." All of Clear Enigma had been in on it. Lindsey must have been, which meant Sierra too. Sierra might have spoken to Kimi.

That's how it went with Hartwell. Everyone knew everyone else. No matter how well something was buried, eventually it came to the surface.

The Clear Enigma fans would dissect every line to decode that song, the same way they'd done with the first version. Someone would blow up grainy video stills to show Rose wasn't wearing the ring. Their high school classmates would unearth everything, assuming Mia herself didn't pour grist into the hopper of the rumor mill.

They reached a crossroad, and Rose hesitated, then chose one. There was no destination at the end of these spaghetti roads. She clenched her hand on the ring on the chain.

We were in high school. What did any of us know? It was all so dramatic back then. Everything seemed so final. Declan had taken a shot at Rose and expected her to forgive him for it. Rose had deflected mockery onto him and wiped it from her own memory through embarrassment. Rose had betrayed a friend to spare herself social isolation. Declan had ignored his sister because he was preening over himself.

"Can't I have changed?" Rose had asked him on the mountain.

"Are you sure she's changed?" Kimi had asked him on the phone five hours later.

But maybe that was the point. Maybe over time, all of them had changed. Kimi had forced change in good ways. She'd changed schools, changed her appearance, changed her focus, even changed her name. Declan had changed with less intentionality, understanding over time that the world was so much larger than the gossip and the single performances. Rose had accepted the isolation by becoming the tomboy in an underground band, but was that change? Or was she changing now by accepting herself?

What did he want to do?

What did he want to do about her?

They reached another street, and Rose stopped. Declan didn't offer a suggestion, and she continued without turning. They could maybe do this all night and eventually stop when they hit the Canadian border. Maybe he'd come up with a way to say something. Maybe he'd come up with what he wanted to say. Maybe she was waiting for him to start, or maybe she thought he was waiting for her.

Except all this speculation meant he wasn't here with Rose. Whatever was going to happen was going to happen here. Now. With her. Sending his brain away into a dozen different conversations they could have meant he wouldn't be here for whatever conversation they eventually did have.

It was time to be fully present. No relayed messages. No mind off in the music.

Rose turned onto another street, one that curved wildly. There were few houses here, all set back from the road and spaced apart. A car approached, passed, left them behind. Peeper frogs started chirping as it grew dark. They ought to get back, but there were a lot of things they ought to have done.

At the next intersection, Rose said, "Oh," and turned decisively up one street. They walked a little faster, and then she took Declan's hand. He wove his fingers through hers. She knew where she was now. He was just accompanying her.

Would she understand if he said he was complicit in what happened with Kimi? Or would she use that as an excuse to absolve herself once more?

Maybe that didn't matter. Maybe he needed to tell her anyway.

Two more turns and they were on the street behind the Gilbert Ridge, at the entrance to the staff parking lot. Wandering without a destination, somehow they'd gotten where they were meant to go.

Sitting on his piano tonight, Rose had sung, "I can't ask his forgiveness. And you know I deserve this."

None of them got what they deserved. Kimi hadn't deserved the bullying. Rose hadn't deserved the cheating. Mia and Travis—well, they did deserve one another.

Rose was silent because she couldn't ask his forgiveness. Could he forgive her?

He could. Did he choose to?

They were standing again by the front entrance of the Gilbert Ridge, and Declan could hear a jazz trio within. If he listened closely enough, he might be able to identify the saxophonist. But they were in there, and he needed to stay out here.

Rose looked up at him, so he took her other hand. The tears in her eyes gleamed in the overhead lights of the parking lot.

She felt solid under his touch, and he grounded himself in the moment. "We're back where we started."

"We covered a lot of territory." Rose looked aside. "I can't fix the past, and I have no right to ask your forgiveness. But if I could make it right, I would."

"I need to make things right too." He lowered his eyes. "I've been selfish. I leaped to conclusions and didn't question them. I was focused on blaming Mia, and then I shifted it to you and wouldn't hear your apology."

Rose looked aside. "You don't have to do this."

He squeezed her hands. "I was so driven by wanting to even the score that I forgot the reasons I was doing it, and who I was doing it for."

Rose said, "And then I undid that too."

"I shouldn't have been looking for revenge in the first place. I'm sorry." Declan braced himself. "We started this whole thing for the wrong reasons, but we can start over for the right ones."

She still wouldn't meet his eyes. "Can you forgive me? For real? Not faking it?"

For real.

He'd had to forgive himself for his own role in Kimi's crisis. It would be hypocritical not to forgive Rose too.

"For real," he said, and then he drew her closer and kissed her. He could forgive her. More than that, he finally wanted to.

EPILOGUE

Rose raised her head because she wasn't finding anything in all this dirt. "Can I have the pinpointer when you're done?"

"I'm done." Declan climbed away from his hole, brushing the dirt off his arms as he approached. "Any idea what you might have?"

"Considering the buckle and porcelain we found, this was probably their bedroom." Rose aimed the pinpointer until it beeped at her. "Ah, I was off to the right."

Declan knelt alongside her, and she thrilled at his nearness. With him this close, she didn't resist inching closer to kiss him.

He side-eyed her. "You didn't need a pinpointer for that."

"My aim for kisses is usually pretty good." She kissed him again, this time longer.

While they dug through the ash layer toward the artifact, Rose breathed deep of the October air, the odor of fallen leaves, and the earthy scent of the dirt pile. The mountain was in flames of a different sort now, with the maples in a riot of reds and oranges, the white birches crowned in gold, and the deciduous pines an array of beige and green.

She scraped her trowel along the edge of the hole, loosening more ash. "We'll never know what caused the fire, or what happened to them afterward."

"The property records are too spotty. I bet they were squatting on the land, probably trapping." Declan pulled out more dirt and ash, dumping it onto the tarp. "All we can see is the fallout from what happened, not the why."

Rose said, "The why is important."

Declan took her hand and squeezed. "It's okay. You can let it go."

He'd said that to her any number of times in the last five months, with a radar sense for when she was remembering what she'd done to Kimi. *You can let it go now*, when the problem all along had been how thoroughly Rose had let it go from the start. Kimi had forgiven her. Rose and Declan had talked it out so often, and Rose had even had a few sessions with a therapist to work on why she was so attuned to others' opinions.

As they dug, Declan said, "I saw Travis, by the way. He's still irritated at me."

"Maybe if you irritate him enough, he'll vanish for good. Mia hasn't shown her face at the diner again. I guess they do have better coffee up the street." The trowel made a new scraping sound, and Rose set it aside to reach with her fingers. "That's the best possible way Mia could have thanked me for not wrecking her wedding with my happiness."

Declan said, "Not wrecking it by not being within fifty miles of it."

"That too." Sean had gone to Travis and Mia's wedding. Corwin had indeed gotten himself uninvited because of the "Second Cousin" song, and Raf bowed out shortly afterward. Which was fine, in the end. Rose had found something better than a catered meal and a cheap wedding favor wrapped up in cheap revenge.

Declan said, "I made a tally last week. Even with skipping theirs, I attended thirty-eight weddings this summer."

Rose paused. Declan had definitely been busy with clients, but that seemed like a lot. "Lucky you."

"Well-paid me. I got to hear plenty of officiants talking about the stars aligning, very little about the hard work it takes to align them."

"And keeping them aligned." Speaking of hard work, she grasped whatever was underground and rocked it to get it loose, then tugged it out. "Button?"

Declan said, "Looks like."

"Kimi has dibs on all buttons. Send her a picture."

Declan took a picture, then dictated into the text, "Rose thinks this round lump of indecipherable metal may be the next member of your button collection."

Rose and Kimi weren't close, but Kimi was willing to give Rose a chance. Mari was more of a holdout, but as of late September she'd allowed Rose into the yard for a cookout.

Rose checked with the pinpointer, which lit up again. "Yeah, the detector thought there was something bigger than a button."

Declan kept hovering, which wasn't his usual practice. Typically they'd work "together" in different zones of the dig site. That was more than enough. For the past five months, they'd fallen into a quiet rhythm of doing things side by side. Her in the dining room at Gilbert's Ridge, listening to him play. Him in her living room, researching historical documents while she practiced on her keyboard.

It felt comfortable. It felt a lot like acceptance.

Declan said, "If you do the hard work of aligning the stars up front, do you have to keep working to keep them aligned? Or do stars just stay where you put them?"

Rose dug toward the second object. "Sierra says the patterns at the start are the patterns you keep following. That's why she hated that we were pretending, and it sickens her that Travis and Mia started with deception."

Declan said, "We were honest about the pretense. And we did learn to communicate."

She kissed him. "We did. Don't let those thirty-eight weddings get to you. Just because everyone makes it seem effortless doesn't mean it's fatal that we had to put in a lot of work."

Declan shook his head. "You were worth the effort. You and I focused a lot on history, though. All those weddings focused on the present and the future, and that made me think about our future."

Rose kept working with the trowel. "What do you think

about our future?"

Declan sat back on his heels. "You and me, a grand piano in the living room, a soundproof practice room in the basement, and a couple of tiny piano prodigies?"

Rose smiled. "I'd like that. Not for a couple of years, though."

Declan nodded. "You still need to go on a world tour with Clear Enigma. Win a few awards, maybe play Fenway Park."

She said, "Honeymoon at the Rock and Roll Hall of Fame?"

Declan gave her a thumbs-up. "Why not? Try to get inducted at the same time as our wedding so we save on the airfare," and she laughed too.

He still wasn't leaving her side, and again it was odd. He seemed nervous. If Declan was worried she was going to louse up the dig, though, he didn't say it, so Rose just kept scraping the dirt. She finally encountered something solid in the ash layer, and this one took a while to manipulate out of the hole. Declan had a go at it, and then Rose again, until finally Declan said, "I think we've got it," and eventually it was Rose who extracted the object. It looked like a long tool, tubular, only with no implement on the end.

Declan exclaimed, "No! Really?" He beamed as she handed it to him. "Rose, this is the best find ever!" He swiveled it to sight along the edge. "I think it's a penny whistle!"

Rose gasped. "They left us their music."

In silence they sat for a few minutes, passing the object between them. It was clogged with dirt and rough with corrosion.

Rose stroked the whistle with her fingertips, afraid it would crumble. "Would it still play?"

"We'll have to try. This is awesome." He looked up. "Since you found something amazing here, I was wondering if you'd help me dig up something amazing over there too."

Why hadn't he just pulled it up himself? "Is it so huge you need two people to lift it?"

"You never know. On the other hand," he added, sounding a little rueful, "you just pulled up the grand prize, so maybe the next object will be a letdown."

He aimed at it with the pinpointer, and she reached into the hole. He'd already loosened quite a bit of the dirt and could have gotten it himself.

Her fingers touched something fuzzy, and she yanked back her hand. "There's something gross in there! It's got fur!"

Declan looked surprised. "I promise there's not. It's too far down."

"You didn't touch what I touched." She reached back in, cautious, and the thing was definitely fuzzy, but firm, and not fuzzy enough to be horrific. She grasped it, and it came free easily.

It was a velvet ring box.

Declan smirked at her, and she raised her eyebrows. "Really?"

The lid sprang open under her fingers, and inside sat a gold ring with a blue solitaire gem. She breathed, "Oh, wow."

Declan took her free hand. "Before now we've only semi-proposed with other people's rings. You deserve one of your own." He gazed into her eyes. "It was a hard road getting to this point, but we're here. I love you. I've loved getting to know you in the present, and it's been worthwhile sifting through the past with you. I want you with me forever in the future. Our future. It will be a future of digging up buttons and playing duets on the same piano, open mic nights and load-outs and wedding performances. Will you marry me?"

Rose kissed him. "I love you too. I want that future together." He slipped the ring from the box and put it onto her finger. "Yes, I will marry you."

He kissed her there, beneath the pine trees in an abandoned homestead. It started with a fire, but it would end with a family.

THANK YOU!

Thank you so much for reading *Faking the Harmony*! I hope you enjoyed reading Declan and Rose's story as much as I enjoyed writing about it.

Hartwell and the Castelton Music School aren't going anywhere. You can read about them in the upcoming Castleton String Quartet Romances, where you'll get a bit more about Corwin's family and one of the secrets they've never disclosed.

Want to hear more? Sign up for my newsletter ("Mondays with Maddie") at http://eepurl.com/dEJjI1 Once a week, I'll send you something cute as well as news about my stories or recommendations of other books you might like.

I'd like to thank the people who helped me with this, including Mallory Crowe from Crowe Covers, my editor Michelle Arnold, and Louise Thygesen for important feedback.

I hope you'll read the next Castelton novel, *Heart of the Violist*.

HEART OF THE VIOLIST

Still reeling from her teacher and father-figure's terminal illness, Ashlyn is struggling toward a brighter future. On the heels of a breakup, Michael is fighting to piece together his past.

What neither realizes is the depth of the secret at the heart of their families, and how prying it open the wrong way may destroy the harmony they're trying to create.

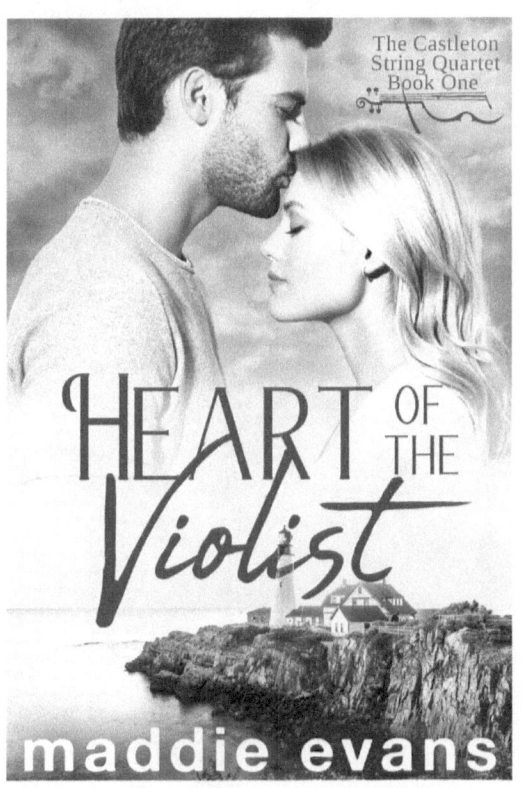